Amazon reviews for \

-Another great read from this author – magical, witty and a thoroughly enjoyable read.

-Wonderful characters and story, which would be enjoyed by all ages.

-Absolute gem of a story – Heartwarming, evocative and with a good splash of humour thrown in.

-The locations are beautifully described; the plot keeps you interested and the characters are sympathetic and believable.

-This the third book written by Susanna Scott and I can wholeheartedly recommend them. On each occasion, work has stopped while I finish reading them.

Susanna Scott lives in a seaside town on the Yorkshire Coast. She loves being out in the Yorkshire countryside, be it Dales, Moors or Coast and finds inspiration for her writing there. She is NOT employed by the Yorkshire tourist board – honest!

Also by Susanna Scott

The Gypsy Caravan

The Winterfell Stone

Weaver's Green

(and for children)

Robin Hood and the Wolfshead Tree

Susanna Scott @yorkshirecoastwriter on Facebook

Susanna Scott -author page on Amazon

ACORN COTTAGE CHRISTMAS

by

Susanna Scott

To Chris and her daughter Lucy for their friendship, encouragement and love.

Chapter 1

December 23ʳᵈ

Sadie Norwood checked the weather forecast again. She realised it wouldn't have changed much since she last checked it two minutes ago, or the time before that – four minutes ago. She could always hope for a Christmas miracle though, couldn't she?

The plan had been to keep Mab's Court open today and even for a few hours in the morning, which would be Christmas Eve. The last was really just to allow the villagers of Brytherstone, set high in the Yorkshire Dales, to get any last minute presents they had forgotten – and to hand out mulled wine and mince pies.

Mab's Court was a courtyard development of retail craft units which Sadie had created five months before in the summer. It stood in the grounds of the newly restored Acorn Cottage and both of them were her dream come true.

It was inside Acorn Cottage that she now stood in a panic. She blinked at the forecast. It *had* changed in the last two minutes – it was even worse than before. Snow, snow and more snow.

If it wasn't for the business, she would gladly have hidden herself away here in the cottage with all the people she cared about nearby. Her aunt, one of the reasons she moved here, was only at the other side of the village of Brytherstone, which was half a mile away from the little country lane she lived on.

All the unit owners though, were hoping for a little last-minute income as Christmas was a good time for the gifts they sold. There were craftsman-made wooden and leather gifts, knitted, crocheted and embroidered clothes and gifts, unique jewellery, stained glass crafts, watercolour artwork and Sadie's own herbal products. There was also Meg's delicious baking and all of the Xmas cakes she had saved for today and tomorrow.

Two of the owners had already cancelled, including Fran and Col's wooden gifts and candle shop. Fran was away visiting her mother and Col would be fetching her back on Christmas Eve. They were also having problems as they had to give up their rented house by March and with Fran being pregnant again with their fourth child (our last one, Col had said, I'm having the snip now!) they had their hands full at the moment.

Sadie sighed – and then thought, it's not the end of the world, is it? She forced a smile onto her face, which probably made her look as though she was in pain. It was at this point that the back door flew open and a man, carrying a box full of wine, started to make his way into the kitchen. He stopped dead at the sight of Sadie's 'smile'.

'Oh dear' he said – calmly, under the circumstances, she thought.

'I'm *not* dreaming of a whiiite Christmaaas' she sang as he laughed and plonked the plonk down on the long wooden kitchen table.

'Where's your romantic soul?' said Raff as he kissed Sadie's cheek. 'Besides, a white Christmas at Acorn Cottage is what you've been dreaming of since you bought this place'

'All this is true' agreed Sadie 'but it's just Mab's Court.'

'Ah yes – I know it's not what you planned but the best laid plans of mice and men etc etc. It's not the end of the world, is it?'

'You've just echoed my exact thoughts' said Sadie, wide eyed.

'It's because I can read your mind *mo chroi.*' He intensified his stare as he looked unflinchingly into her eyes.

'Don't you come your gypsy ways with me sir' she laughed as he grinned back. He turned to go back through the door and then said over his shoulder,

'Ali and George going to make it for Christmas?'

'I don't know yet. We're keeping in touch about the train situation.'

'Oh well, I'll fetch the second box of wine anyway.'

'Are you saying my best friend drinks a lot?' she asked, eyebrows raised. A laugh was the only answer as he shut the door behind him.

Sadie moved across to the French windows so she could watch him walk up the long garden to go past the gypsy caravan to his own log cabin home.

She had met Raff Maguire, short for Raphael, when she first came up here last Spring. He had at first seemed a moody and bad-tempered Heathcliff type but as he thought she was breaking in to the then empty Acorn Cottage, she supposed he could be excused. He had turned out to be kind, loyal and a good friend. And a little more than that as time went on.

Also, let it not be forgotten, he was devastatingly handsome. Tall, slim but muscled, his almost black hair reached over his collar and his blue eyes with his dark brows and long black lashes showed his Celtic gypsy origins. Although his mother had been a member of the minor Scottish aristocracy so he seemed to have that bearing and inbuilt confidence too.

She watched him now, disappearing to the left into the clearing where his grandfather's gypsy caravan stood. Sadic closed her eyes at the memory of the nights they had spent there together, looking out at the moon and stars with nothing but the hoot of an owl to disturb them.

The nights they spent together now were divided between the cottage and the luxurious log cabin he had built on his own land, with the occasional, magical night spent in their 'special place'.

There was no doubt they loved one another. This thought still gave Sadie butterflies in her stomach as it was a fairly new relationship and she still didn't think she deserved him, no matter how many times he told her. This was compounded by how their relationship could be defined. He didn't want to leave his cabin and she wouldn't leave Acorn Cottage, which had belonged to her ancestors long before Sadie bought it. They were both still clinging to their freedom, both reluctant to let go and commit fully. It seemed to work at the moment though as they were both happy. Deliriously so, in Sadie's case.

Her mobile phone rang and brought her back to the present. She looked at the name – Drew, the artist. It was another cancellation as he had the furthest to drive and was worried about his old van getting there. She reassured him it was fine and she might have to cancel today and tomorrow anyway. She would have to go down to Mab's Court to see if anyone had turned up. The ones who lived in the village might but it was debatable.

She thought about taking Whisky the Cairn terrier, who had changed loyalties from her aunt to herself – and Raff's sheepdog Bran – but thought Whisky might disappear up to his ears. They were both fast asleep next to the Aga anyway and it would take more than a couple of dog treats to shift them in this weather, she reckoned.

The back door opened again and this time Raff and his box of alcohol were accompanied by a flurry of snow, which flew into the Aga-warmed kitchen to disappear forever.

'Snowing again?' asked Sadie, unnecessarily.

'And you should see the sky over Mab's Wood' he said, 'it's heavy with more snow to come.'

'I'm going to walk down to the Court to open the herb unit and see what anyone else has to say, if any of the others have turned up at all.'

Joanna, the vicar's wife had wanted to come up but Thomas phoned earlier, saying his wife had been ill this morning, probably something she ate yesterday so he was banning her from coming. This had made Sadie laugh as Thomas was very mild-mannered and if Joanna had wanted to come up, she would have.

'I'm going over to Gressleigh to pick the turkey up, as well as the ham, pork and a few other things we might need. Can you think of anything?' Raff said, not even stopping for a warming cup of tea.

'No, I've got everything else on order at the village but – be careful won't you? I don't know what the main roads are like but the B-roads won't be good.'

'Stop worrying woman, the Land Cruiser won't let me down, it loves weather like this.' He pulled her towards him to give her a hug , then looked into her gentle green eyes with a smile. He took in the Pre-Raphaelite auburn hair which tumbled round her shoulders and put out his hand to stroke it.

'You be careful walking down there too' he smiled 'Wear your skis'

'I'm strapping tennis rackets to my wellies as we speak' she shouted after him.

Chapter 2

The snow was much thicker than she had realised. The only time she had poked her nose outside was to let Whisky out of the back door first thing and as he hadn't disappeared immediately under the snow, she thought it wasn't too bad. The cottage must have been sheltering the back terrace.

The long driveway led down to Mab's Court and its small car park on the right with Mab's Wood beyond it, a small field's width away. Just below the Court was a country lane which, if you turned left at the end, joined the road down the hill into the village of Brytherstone.

The snow was still swirling around her as she came up to her shop 'Healing Herbs'. It was looking forlorn with snow piled up against the window. Her mobile rang again, a sort of disjointed noise as though it were ringing underwater. She hoped the network wouldn't go down.

'Hello Meg?' she could hear her worried voice on the other end but it wasn't very clear and sounded like she was twittering. Which to be fair, would be par for the course for Meg. She could hear her trying to shout louder.

'I don't know – can you hear me? – I don't know whether to bring this baking today. Em said -I hope you can hear this – Em said she'd give me a lift. Or should I freeze it? Did you get that? Should I freeze it? It doesn't seem worth it if no one turns up to buy it and I'd have to bring it all back again. I've got a few orders but I can ring them and tell them to come here instead? What do you think? Do you think anyone will come? Can you hear me?'

Meg hadn't given Sadie chance to answer as, though she couldn't be certain because of the mobile reception, she was fairly sure that Meg hadn't taken a breath throughout that speech.

'Don't worry Meg' she shouted as clearly as she could. 'Don't come in. Not sure anyone else is here anyway. Weather bad and set to get much worse. Some for Christmas day would be good, especially your Christmas cakes.'

'Oh they'll keep anyway and I've done you an extra special one for your first Christmas at Acorn Cottage anyway. Oh!' Meg paused. 'I was going to keep that a secret.'

Sadie laughed quietly to herself.

'I'd rather know so I have the anticipation beforehand.' She grinned before putting the phone back in her pocket.

Meg was her Aunt Em's best friend and two more opposite personalities you couldn't find. Meg was gentle, scatty, plump and fantastic with food. Em had a caustic wit, an uncompromising personality and a culinary talent which kept people away from her meals in droves, when she actually bothered to cook at all.

She was, however, a nationally renowned sculptor – limestone being her preferred medium as it was readily available locally in the Yorkshire Dales. She had also, much to everyone's surprise – especially hers – got married in the autumn, in her mid-sixties. She had the energy of a ten year old and the same lack of respect for authority as a teenager.

She had married her long-term 'friend', James – properly known as James Fitzherbert, Earl of Gressleigh and lived with him at Winterhill Lodge, just out of the village at the far side. Next door was Winterhill Manor which belonged to James before the overheads became too much and he donated it to the National Trust. Em was still a Norwood though, like Sadie. Sadie loved her to bits. James too as a more likeable and thoroughly 'nice' man you couldn't hope to meet.

Sadie came back to reality as two figures emerged from the leathercraft unit. Ian, who did the leatherwork and his wife Dilly who made embroidered gifts and tapestry panels. They looked cold and miserable with their coats pulled tightly round them and their matching bobble hats pulled low over their ears.

'I think this might be a waste of time Sadie. We only passed a couple of cars on the way here and nobody has been near us yet. As for tomorrow…'

Christmas Eve. All the plans they'd had to hand out Christmas cake, mince pies and mulled wine to get a party atmosphere going .

Perhaps next year, thought Sadie, refusing to be defeated.

'It's okay Ian, get yourselves home. The weather is set to be even worse so perhaps we could just look forward to our January 2nd re-opening instead?'

'That's the spirit' said Ian, slapping her a little too hard on her back, while Dilly said,

'You can't imagine how glad I am to hear you say that.'

'I'm just going to check my shop while I'm here then will go into Brytherstone to collect my orders. What's the road in there like?'

Ian frowned and looked up at the snow which was now being driven by a gathering wind.

'Passable at the moment' he said 'but looking at this little lot, not for much longer.'

Sadie smiled weakly and thought of Raff travelling to Gressleigh, the nearest market town.

'Well look, if I don't see you before – and I probably won't – have a lovely Christmas and I'll see you in the New Year.'

Ian and Dilly answered in the same vein then they all hugged before they locked up and got into their car.

Another call on the mobile - Shelley this time and she possibly would have had the most to gain in the way of small last minute Christmas presents with her hand-made jewellery. Again, Sadie felt like she had to apologise for putting her off but Shelley seemed relieved. She was the landlord's daughter from The Falling Stone pub in the village. She had just moved in with the local book shop owner and was probably as excited over their first Christmas together as Sadie was for her and Raff's.

That's why she had wanted this Christmas to be perfect. This snow might just scupper their plans though. It was looking increasingly unlikely that Ali, George and the two boys were going to make it as they lived in Harrogate, nearly forty miles away.

Just as she was walking back towards her driveway, she heard the crunching of tyres on snow and the next minute, Thomas's 'inadequate for the weather' old hatchback drove into the courtyard. Or maybe slid into it would be a better way of putting it. She saw Thomas's piggy eyes grow wide behind his gold-rimmed spectacles, as he corrected the skid. Joanna's face didn't change, it was calm and serene as usual. Sadie went up to the car as it finally halted.

Thomas had been a childhood friend from the school holidays that she had spent up here with Em. He hadn't changed much at all, in looks or personality.

'What are you doing here?' asked Sadie, frowning as she looked at Joanna. Thomas answered for her.

'She insisted she felt much better. She didn't want to let you down. Or anyone else who might be mad enough to come up here in this weather. She was going to *walk* up!' Thomas finished incredulously.

'Might have been safer?' Joanna said quietly with an ironic smile on her face.

Sadie explained that now she had seen how bad it was and with no chance of it getting better for Christmas Eve, she was going to let the remaining owners know that everything was cancelled now, until New Year.

'So sorry Joanna. How are you feeling now?' asked Sadie.

'I'm fine, honestly' answered Joanna.

'So she says but she really wasn't well when she got up. It's just so…*Joanna*, to insist on not letting people down.'

'It is' agreed Sadie with a smile. If she could have picked the archetypal village vicar and his wife, Thomas and Joanna would be her choice. They were such good, unassuming people.

'I'd ask you if you wanted to come up to the cottage for a cup of tea but…'

Thomas shook his head.

'I think I'd better concentrate on getting us home in one piece, don't you?' he said with a fond glance at his wife.

'That would definitely be a good idea' laughed Joanna.

Sadie watched as he executed an elegant spin in the courtyard which would have made John Curry jealous before managing to turn right and down into the driveway.

As Sadie walked back up to the cottage, she sent a group message to the Mab's Court shopkeepers saying Christmas was cancelled.

After collecting her handbag and changing into her walking boots – she just couldn't drive in wellies – she left Whisky and Bran in the warmth and got into her own 'inadequate in the snow' car to fetch her Christmas orders from the village. She wasn't too confident at driving in the snow herself and she just hoped that her car wouldn't be performing the Skater's Waltz on its way into the village.

Chapter 3

Sadie's mobile went off again as soon as she had kicked her boots off onto the mat.

'Hello? Ali?. Yes I can just about hear you although you sound very quiet and that is SO not you – it's the mobile reception.' She laughed as her normally loud, funny and enthusiastic friend pretended to be affronted. 'Oh no – I thought you'd be cancelling because of the weather forecast but I secretly hoped you'd make it. No, please don't go to the local garage and hire a family size snowmobile for you all! No, I think Santa may be needing his sleigh for other purposes than transporting my mad best friend to the middle of the Yorkshire Dales. We will hopefully get together in the New Year. Yes, love you too and lots of love to George and the boys as well. I'll ring you over Christmas.'

She put the phone back in her pocket with a feeling of disappointment. Plans for her first Christmas here had definitely involved Ali. Perversely, she was glad too as the trains were cancelled now on that route so it would have been a bit risky anyway. She would rather they were safe. Besides, it would be their first Christmas in their new house in Harrogate after George had become a partner in the local doctor's practice, so they would still enjoy it together as a family.

Now that the original idea of working today and tomorrow morning had gone out of the window, Sadie realised that she had more time then she thought to prepare for Christmas Day. There were presents to finish wrapping and food to collect and prepare. She had hand-made Raff's present but was going through agonies now in case he didn't like it. Was it really his thing? Had she made it because *she* liked the idea rather than because he would? He would certainly pretend to like it as he wouldn't hurt her feelings for the world. All she could say with any certainty was that every part of it had been made with love.

She looked out the window to see the snow being driven against the windows. She had better not delay going for her orders in the village. First though, the sleeping hounds had to go out, whether they wanted to or not. Not – would be Sadie's guess in Whisky's case.

She called them both. Bran put his head up then hesitantly padded across the floor. Whisky didn't even stir, although he opened one eye when he didn't think Sadie was watching and quickly closed it again when he saw she was.

'Alright, we'll go without you then' she said to him as her and Bran went out of the door. One thing Whisky hated more than being cold was being left out of things. Next minute, he appeared at the open door and looked to his right, where Sadie and Bran were waiting for him to do just what he had done.

'*Doggone it*' thought Whisky, '*foiled again!*' and his eyes registered total disdain as he stepped gingerly past them into the snow, his whisky-coloured fur soon being covered in giant flakes of snow.

They walked as far as the caravan, which they checked. The inside was watertight, or snow-tight in this case – but even the brightly coloured furnishings now looked dark against the brightness of the snow. It would only take a couple of the oil lamps to be switched on and the wood burner flickering to make all the difference. It might even be too cold in there for Raff, who could usually put up with all sorts of weather and temperatures.

The dogs both made for their beds near the Aga again when they got back, only moving to roll over a little as Sadie struggled to towel them dry.

I don't know about a dog and his master, thought Sadie, but I know who the masters are around here.

*

The journey into the village hadn't been too bad, although she had done a sideways skid into the verge. Luckily she managed to drive it off the verge and into the village without further incident and parked without actually seeing where the road ended and the pavement began. She wouldn't risk moving again and would just cart everything back to the car from each shop.

She got out of the car just as the snow whipped up a storm then knocked on the door of the nearest house – Church View Cottage. This place had been her grandparent's house when they worked for the Winterhill estate and then passed on to Em when Sadie's mum, Em's sister, moved down to the city, thankful to be away from country life.

Em had lived there all her life and Sadie spent many happy Easters and Summers with her aunt. There, instead of being controlled as she was at home, she was given the freedom to be a carefree child – and she had never stopped being grateful to Em for this. Sadie's mum and dad now lived in America and were only in touch occasionally. They had never been close.

When Em married James and moved to Winterhill Lodge, the cottage became Meg's home and it was a flustered Meg, ruddy-faced and with her cardigan buttoned up wrongly, who answered the door now.

'Oh Sadie! I was just wondering how to get some of these things up to you. I've frozen a lot but there's still loads. There might not be room in Em's car tomorrow with there being three of us. I'm baking fresh bread first thing in the morning but the rest is ready to go up. Apart from your cake, I'll bring that later.'

'Don't worry Meg, that's why I've called. I can put your stuff on the back seat and the rest of my shopping in the boot..'

'You're a life-saver' said Meg gratefully 'and always so calm too.'

Not on the inside, thought Sadie, thinking once again that she would be glad when Raff was home.

They loaded it into the car, then Sadie set off for last minute things from the newsagents down the road. Will Pike, the newsagent's son, was serving in the shop today.

'Mum and dad have gone into Gressleigh to the butchers but they've just phoned to say they'll be late back as the roads are getting bad so they're taking it slowly.

Sadie's heart sank but really, Raff was the most capable person she knew and seemed to manage in most situations that were thrown at him.

'There's a blues band on at the pub tonight, it's Smokey Blue from over the dale at Winterfell, so they should get here okay. Are you going?'

'I think there might be too much to do at home but I've seen them before and they're really good, so never say never.'

Next, she picked up two large boxes of organic veg and fruit from Singh's shop and he very kindly carried one back to the car with Sadie. Her heart was in her mouth though as he skidded and all the onions, cabbage and potatoes in the box jumped up into the air before regaining their equilibrium at the same time as Mr Singh.

Archers had her sparkling wine ready for her and she popped next door to Dawsons to pick up a present that had been left there for her. The last call was to see if an expected parcel had been delivered but she knew the answer before she got there. She would make alternative arrangements online.

She made her unsteady way back to the car. She felt much better walking in snow than driving in it, as the snow was getting so thick it would cushion any falls she had. In a car, however, there was the thought of it getting stuck in a snowdrift or getting damaged, with the ensuing insurance claims – or even going out of control and ending up on its roof.

It was with these happy thoughts in her head that Sadie made her tentative way back up the hill, wishing that Raff was at home safe and sound.

Chapter 4

The night was drawing in. The dark clouds had a purple tinge to them and a strange yellow sky heralded yet more snow.

There was still no sign of Raff. Sadie was trying not to call him as he might have been concentrating on negotiating snow-covered roads but it was getting to the stage now where she couldn't settle to anything.

She had cleared up, wrapped up the few presents she hadn't already wrapped and done all the preparation she could do at this stage. All Meg's baking, including mince pies, sausage rolls, pies and various sweet delights was all put away in cupboards, fridges and freezers. The other food would have to be prepared tomorrow – Christmas Eve. The rest of her time had been spent on deciding what to wear on Christmas Day and in making sure all the decorations were in place and looking their best.

She looked above her at the thick wooden beams which set the tone for this early English kitchen. The holly and ivy garlands which her and Raff had pinned up there the day before, still looked fresh with no sign of any berries dropping or leaves drooping.

There were similar garlands in the dining room, where everyone would eat at the long oak table. In there were also swags of pine branches, pine cones still attached, above the dresser and the old fireplace. Fairy lights were pinned around the French doors leading to the terrace outside, to add to the illusion of a fairyland Christmas and to mirror the ones on the very large Christmas tree at the other end of the room.

Ever since she had moved here in the summer, she had pictured exactly where her Christmas tree was going to go. Now she knew she had got it right as she surveyed the tree. Good Housekeeping or Country Living magazines couldn't have made it look any better than she and Raff had. Sadie smiled as she thought of him on the stepladder as she'd passed him the fairy to place at the top of the tree.

'Really?' he'd said, 'a fairy?'

She had nodded as he climbed up the steps with an exaggerated reluctance in his movements. She laughed at his expression as he had gingerly placed the white, lacy object on the pinnacle of the tree, its red rosebud mouth had the lipstick veering off to one side of the pottery lips as though it had been put on after too many thimblefuls of fairy mead. The bright blue painted eyes stared back at him as he gave the white fake-fur cape a last pat down and reached terra firma again with a pained expression on his face.

It looked good though and it was the first Christmas tree they had decorated together. Sadie fervently hoped there would be many more.

She glanced across at the grandmother clock in the opposite corner to the tree. Frowning, she picked up her mobile phone. Driving or not, she had to know that he was alright. Then she put it down again as she thought that her ringing him on an icy road might cause things *not* to be alright. She was just weighing things up when she heard a yappy bark and a deeper bark and as she ran to the front of the house to look through the windows, she heard the kitchen door open at the back.

She dashed back through to see Raff smiling but looking worried.

'I tried to phone you but the weather is making the network very patchy. It's bad enough anyway with all the hills and dales round here. You weren't worried, were you?'

'Not really' she lied through her teeth while resisting the urge to burst into tears of relief. 'I can't believe I didn't hear you approach though as I've been listening out for you for ages.'

This statement immediately made nonsense of her 'unconcerned' stance.

'It's the snow' he replied, 'it's muffling all sound. It's strangely silent out there.'

He came across and enveloped her in a protective hug. His height meant that he could easily plant many kisses on the top of her head before smoothing her hair away from her face. He looked into her eyes with the intensity that always made Sadie's stomach flip before slowly – and deliciously – touching his lips to hers, lightly at first, then much harder. They pulled away reluctantly with an unstated promise for later and got on with the mundane task of putting the shopping away.

'I thought Dodos were extinct?' Raff said, holding up the fresh turkey, which indeed looked like it might feed the five thousand.

'I thought Thomas and Joanna were coming but they decided to stay at home *and* I had figured in Ali and the crew but now because of the snow, that's four more we won't have now' replied Sadie, pulling a sad face.

'It's a shame they can't come but they might not have been able to get back, even if they made it here. At least we'll be sure the booze will last us for a couple of days.'

'Raff!' Sadie said in mock disapproval as she knew he was fond of Ali and her family. Besides, there was a time when Sadie could have matched Ali drink for drink.

'The Dodo won't fit' said Raff, looking for all the world like he was trying to fit a camel through the eye of a needle.

There followed a changeover of fridge shelves, a transfer of relevant foods to a cold larder shelf and a final shove to get Dotty the

Dodo into the fridge, which caused much hilarity. In all honesty, as they'd given it a name, Sadie wasn't sure she could eat turkey for Christmas dinner now.

'I called in at Pike's shop on the way back. Firelighters and matches.'

'Got some.' Sadie threw back.

'Is this the end?' Raff hammed it up, 'is there no communication between us anymore?'

'The more matches, the merrier' laughed Sadie. 'Anyway, whatever happened to your skills of lighting fires with a couple of flints and some dry twigs.'

'It went when I stopped saying "Ugg" and learnt to stand upright. Anyhow, there are a million candles to light.'

'This is true' she smiled.

Sadie loved flickering lights – as well as fairy lights, subdued lighting, moonlight, starlight and – well, the power of light. Candles just made everything so warm and welcoming, almost like being in your own fairy tale.

Fran, Col's wife, made candles at the unit she shared with her husband's woodcrafts. Sadie had bought up nearly her whole supply of fragrant candles – church, scented, tealights, tapered – especially when she heard that they wouldn't be able to open up today and tomorrow. She hoped they would get back okay from Fran's mother's in this weather. The blues band were coming from the same direction tonight to play at The Falling Stone, so it might not be too bad.

'Smokey Blue are playing at the pub tonight, mad fools that they are' mentioned Raff, out of the blue, as Sadie's eyes widened.

'I wish you'd stop reading my mind' she laughed.

'It's the only way I'll ever understand you, *mo chridhe*' he grinned back. 'Do you fancy going?'

Sadie's mouth hung open.

'You are joking aren't you? Have you seen it out there?'

'It hasn't snowed for a while now and if Smokey Blue can drive over from Winterfell, I'm sure we can manage to walk down.'

'Walk?' howled Sadie incredulously.

'Better than driving. Don't fancy digging the car out of a snowdrift at midnight but I can put up with wet and icy trousers from the knee down. Come on *cailin*, get wrapped up. We've done everything and we have a spare night. Relax!'

A couple of hours later after having eaten, dragged the dogs out against their will for five minutes, warmed up with a shower and put five layers of clothing on, they stood in the kitchen, ready to put their walking boots on.

Sadie looked at Raff, which was one of her favourite pastimes. She still couldn't believe she was with this man. His black hair shone in the lamp light; his chiselled jaw set as he concentrated on tying the laces. His whole physique just made Sadie weak with longing. His lips…well, totally irresistible, as she proved by going up to him and kissing them passionately.

Raff raised his eyebrows and smiled lazily.

'Or we could just stay in tonight?' He started to take his long, black woollen coat off again.

'Oh no blues boy, let's get down there and enjoy the music. Just to show I'm not a wimp. And there's plenty of time for 'staying in' later.' She grinned and gave him an exaggerated wink.

Chapter 5

The walk - or slither – down to the village pub had been 'interesting', the result of which being that Sadie now had a large wet patch on her derriere and Raff had a stupid grin on his face.

However, he led her over to the roaring fire where she stood with her back to it, steam rising from her, hoping without expectation that it would be dry in minutes.

Surprisingly, the place was packed. With it being bad weather, Sadie hadn't expected this many people to turn out but it was as full as she'd ever seen it. Conversations merged into other conversations and created a sociable buzz throughout the bar. The saturnine landlord, Jez Cobb, handed out the drinks and his daughter Shelley had been drafted in to help. Jez never cracked a smile but had a wonderful dry humour that wasn't immediately apparent. He also did a lot for charity and tonight's entertainment was in aid of a local children's hospice – another reason for the good attendance.

People shouted greetings to them, used to seeing them together as a couple by now. Joanna's friend Betty was there with her husband Paul, who was a music teacher at the school and sometimes entertained everyone on the pub piano. More honky tonk than Chopin in this case. They came over to talk to them.

'Didn't think you'd have ventured down that hill tonight' said Betty.

'It's venturing back up that worries me more' laughed Sadie. 'One step up and two slides backwards all the way.'

'At least this time you'll probably fall forwards and have a wet patch on your front to match this one' said Raff, mercilessly turning Sadie round to reveal the still very wet patch there. 'Are the band here?'

'Yes, down at the far end' replied Paul. 'They came early so they were sure of getting here and Jez offered them a couple of rooms to crash down in if they were stuck here. They have families though – the double bassist is a friend of mine – so they'll try to get home I imagine.

As if on cue, the first strings were plucked on the guitar and as the rest of the band joined in, the singer's low, gravelly voice wound its way towards them singing Rory Gallagher's 'A Million Miles Away'.

The clamour and movement increased as the evening went on with village voices joining in with the more upbeat songs. The band didn't want to leave it too late setting off back so they started slowing down after an hour. Mellow tunes replaced the noisier ones and a sleepy silence hung over the audience for the last song. As the strains of Gary Moore's 'Midnight Blues' reached them, Raff stood behind Sadie, his arms around her as she leant back against his shoulder, both of them swaying to the hypnotic, husky voice of the singer.

Then it was finished and after a loud round of applause and cheers, the band rushed to get their things loaded up in the van and begin their journey home.

Raff and Sadie finished their drinks and said goodbye to everyone, then wearing hats, coats, scarves, gloves and a look of resignation, they launched themselves out into the cold night. It still wasn't snowing but the snow drifts, reaching up a foot or more against the house walls on one side of the street, showed little sign of thawing.

'I'm not looking forward to this' moaned Sadie, her teeth chattering with the cold.

'Imagine you're lost in the deserted wastelands of Siberia, walking forever, directionless, slowly freezing to death' said Raff reflectively.

Sadie turned slowly to face him with a hard stare.

'And that's supposed to make me feel better?' she said incredulously.

'No but just imagine how happy and relieved you'll feel in that case when Acorn Cottage with its welcoming lights, comes into view after only twenty minutes walking' he said seriously.

Sadie's eyebrows shot up.

'Well, I suppose there is some sort of weird, psychological basis for that statement then.' She shook her head and they smiled at each other as a white van came out of the car park driveway.

'Good luck on the drive back' said Raff to the bassist who was driving.

'I think we'll need it' he said, nodding up to his right in the direction they were heading. 'Can we give you a lift?'

Raff checked Sadie who didn't look sure.

'It'll hold the road better; you'll provide it with a bit more ballast' the driver said wryly.

'What are you trying to say here?' laughed Sadie as she looked down at her normally svelte figure, now encased in many layers and a what looked like a tog.15 duvet for a coat.

He laughed back but then added 'You'd have to get in the back with the instruments and sound equipment though.'

'That does it, I'd rather do a belly flop in the snow than be knocked unconscious by a flying amplifier' concluded Sadie.

'But thanks for asking' smiled Raff. 'Take care.'

They all shouted their farewells and did the thumbs up sign before trundling slowly up the road towards Winterfell.

The trail back was laborious and even through thick woollen socks and strong leather walking boots, Sadie's feet were freezing and her fingers were slowly going numb too.

'This felt like a reasonable idea a few hours ago and now it feels like a costly mistake. The cost being most of my fingers dropping off' she whined.

'Such a drama queen.' Raff rolled his eyes. 'Put one hand in my pocket and the other in yours.'

'Can't' she said with newly-surfaced teenage angst 'I need one arm to cling on to you and the other arm to hold out for balance.'

'Come on, we're nearly there.'

Sadie looked sideways at this statement from Raff.

'I am aware' she said 'that the same phrase has been spoken, since time immemorial, by parents to fractious young children when they're whingeing.'

'I'm saying nothing' said Raff innocently.

'Not if you value your life, you're not.' Sadie scowled and then, belying the words, they stopped for a hug and a frozen-lipped kiss before they went on.

As they were halfway up the driveway, Acorn Cottage came into view. Lights from the hallway lent a suffused light to the downstairs windows and an old-fashioned coach lamp at each side of the cottage, shone through the night sky to make it look Christmassy. Adding to this effect were twinkling lights hung over the porch and over the box bush pots at each corner of the porch.

The moon shone down on the stone, making it a silver-grey rather than its usual mellow golden colour and the snow on the tiled roof was so thick that Santa's sleigh was assured of a comfortable landing. Sadie sighed happily.

'Told you.' Raff beamed, catching her expression.

'It was worth crossing Siberia for' she smiled. 'I do *love* Acorn Cottage.'

'You don't say' he laughed then his face grew more thoughtful. 'I'm sorry your first Christmas here will be without your best friend and her family. I know you wanted it to be perfect but even if it ends up just being us two, it will be just as perfect. For me anyway.'

Raff looked down at his feet, he wasn't given to quasi-emotional speeches. Being the strong, silent type, emotion embarrassed him but luckily for Sadie, he was capable of feeling it, if not expressing it. She hugged him again.

'It would be perfect for me too' she said, snuggling into his shoulder.

As they came round the house to the back door, Sadie said,

'So you don't think Em and James will make it either?'

'I'm sure that if Em is determined to come, then Em will – and James will move heaven and earth and ten tons of snow to get her here. Besides, on a more selfish note, they're bringing Meg and she's got more food so they'd better.'

Sadie surveyed the large kitchen as they entered. It was so warm and welcoming with its subtle yellow lighting in all corners or niches – and the under-counter lighting that gave an added glow to the room. She didn't turn the overhead light on as it would disturb the magic. The Aga threw out much-needed heat and they both made for it, holding their frozen hands over the top. Whisky and Bran jumped up and greeted them as they came in as if they actually had been lost in Siberia for weeks, then made happy whimpering noises as they wrapped themselves round their legs.

Raff reached up and pressed a button attached to a wire to the left and immediately all the fairy lights twinkled into being on the garlands hung from beams around the room.

'Oh' Sadie breathed 'isn't it lovely?'

Raff grinned at her rapt expression then moved over to the worktop.

'Brandy?' he asked.

'Hot chocolate?' she countered.

'Hot chocolate with brandy in it' he said finally.

'Perfect' smiled Sadie.

Chapter 6

Christmas Eve

Sadie stirred in the night and the next thing, she was suddenly awake, her brain full of everything she had to do today. She looked at the clock on the bedside table – 5.35 a.m. She groaned, it was too early and now she would have to get another hour or two's sleep while her brain was in overdrive.

She slid out of bed quietly so as not to disturb Raff, who still slept silently beside her. She tiptoed over to the window and pulled a curtain back. The snow was falling again. Not heavily but steadily. There was virgin snow in the front garden, devoid of any doggy paw and stray fox marks or deer trails. She put her head against the pane and saw that their human footsteps had been erased so there must have been quite a covering since last night. She shivered and slid back into the bed, turning to snuggle up to Raff. He turned towards her.

'Oh, sorry I woke you.'

'I was awake.'

She had forgotten how lightly he slept – like a cat.

'Has it snowed again?' he asked. He must have heard her go over to the window, no matter how quiet she was.

'Yes and it's still snowing. I love snow when everyone is safe inside, looking out at it. It looks so lovely. Em says that sometimes they get cut off here when it's bad though and Winterfell, over in the next dale is just the same. You can't help but worry. I *did* want a white Christmas, but maybe not *this* white' she whispered.

'Why worry, there's nothing you can do about it so try and rid your mind of anxiety. You know that Ali and George are safe at home. Em, James and Meg will be here later in the Land Rover, which can manage this snow with relative ease. If not, I'll get Seth from the village to fetch them on the tractor. I reckon he could be out with the snow plough attachment in the village today anyway because he'll want to clear the way from his farm to the pub.'

They both chuckled. Seth's capacity for the local ale was famous.

'And when Meg gets here, there will be enough provisions to last for a ten day snow siege, so – you're right, I will stop worrying.'

'My worry is that you won't have enough candles.' Raff said with supreme irony as she had bought enough to light up every room in Buckingham Palace. He dodged the pillow she flicked at him. She sat up and looked at the clock.

'Do you think it's too early to get up yet?' she said, although she knew Raff was an early riser, usually leaving her still fast asleep in bed.

'Mm, a bit. Can you think of anything we can do while we wait?'

He smiled lazily at her as he pulled her back down towards him.

*

Sadie's wholemeal toast and honey breakfast was eaten on the go and lunch was forgotten as she moved between each surface of the kitchen. She had made stuffing balls which were now in the fridge and a large baking tin of the traditional stuffing Meg had shown her, with fresh sage, roughly sliced onion, breadcrumbs and an obscene amount of butter.

The batter for the Yorkshire puddings was made and in the fridge too, again, according to Meg's instructions as she said it is better for keeping in the fridge overnight. Although not part of a traditional Christmas dinner, James and Raff would probably revolt if they didn't have them with a roast dinner.

She was now preparing the veg and waiting for Em et al. Em had phoned her to say that they were setting off at 1p.m. and if they weren't there by 2p.m. could she send Bran and Whisky down with a large wheelbarrow tied behind them and a small keg of brandy strapped to their collars.

Raff had peeled a mountain of potatoes and had tried to take the dogs for a long walk through Mab's Wood for Bran, at least, to work some energy off. Border collies never seemed to get tired and were still bouncy after a good walk. Not so with Whisky.

'Come on you two' he had called to the two dogs, sleepy with the warmth, as they were settled into their usual place next to the Aga.

They both looked like they would have to be forcibly removed but Bran had trotted over obediently to his master, while Whisky just twitched an ear. To be fair, there had been a blizzard raging for more than an hour and it had only just calmed down a little.

'Come on you lazy pooch' smiled Raff, 'it will do you good.'

What? I should coco! thought Whisky. *Traipsing in five foot of freezing cold white stuff will do me more good than another forty winks in the warmth? I don't **think** so!*

'I should give up Raff, his delicate little paws aren't made for deep snow.'

Delicate? My paws are very macho, I'll have you know. Still not going though.

Sadie laughed at Whisky's pained expression.

'I cleared a path down to Brighid earlier on, so I'll drag him down as far as there when I get back' and he left with a puzzled Bran who couldn't understand why Whisky wouldn't like to play 'snuffling in the snow' with him.

Sadie finished slicing the carrots and wiped her hands on her fifties-style apron. She filled up the large stove- top, whistling kettle to put on the Aga to boil slowly for when Raff was back, then went to look out of the window.

Brighid. The statue stood there in the snow, looking as benign as ever. Brighid was a triple goddess of hearth and home, the flame of dawn and of healing. She had been present in all Sadie's childhood visits to Brytherstone, in the form of Gaia. A small figure on her bedroom dressing table at Em's.

When Em decided to carve an almost life-size stone statue of Gaia for Sadie's 'Welcome to Brytherstone' housewarming present, it had been made as a fountain, with the fine spray coming from the triangular stone she held in her cupped hands.

After Ned, the gardener, had found a small gold amulet of the goddess in her garden, more research was done by Thomas, who had written 'The History of Brytherstone' and, unusually for a vicar, was interested in pagan deities.

It turned out that Gaia was actually Brighid, identified by the flame of dawn she held in her hands and the cloak that fell to her ankles. The name Brytherstone itself was a corruption of Brighid's Stone.

When Em thought she was carving Gaia, she had made the water come from the triangular stone. After a quick adjustment when they discovered her real identity, the water now came, incongruously, from a flame. Which was a talking point if nothing else.

Sadie dragged on her wellies and reached for her coat. She then lifted Whisky up bodily, to his obvious disgust and planted him down halfway up the path. She set off towards the statue as Whisky, a mutinous expression on his face, refused to move.

Sadie believed that Brighid protected this house after 'seeing' her for a few seconds in the middle of the knot garden where the fountain had been built. She hadn't been remotely spiritual before she came here but after that experience – and after learning that her ancestors were known as witches – she had become a believer of sorts.

Of course, her ancestors were healers, not witches who flew on broomsticks. The restored knot garden was believed to be where Agnes Norwood had her herb garden to grow all her medicinal plants and where Sadie now grew her own herbs.

Agnes's granddaughter Sarah had handwritten, in the late sixteenth century, the 'Book of Healing'. It was as big as a family bible and full of Agnes's old remedies and recipes, balms and poultices, which did indeed look and read like an ancient book of spells. The Norwoods were a strong, matriarchal family and always used the Norwood name instead of taking their husband's names.

Sadie reached Brighid and stared up at her in silent communion.

Thank you for guiding me to this village Brighid and to my real family and my friends. Thank you for helping me find my forever home in Acorn Cottage – and thank you for helping me find Raff, the love of my life.

She realised as she opened her eyes that the snow was coming down heavily again and the sky was purple. As she turned back towards the cottage, she held on to the solid gold amulet Ned had found. Raff had it cleaned and put on a gold chain for her and she wore it every day.

She found Whisky gazing longingly up at the back door with his back resolutely turned to her. If he was human, he would be tapping his foot impatiently. Going inside, she kicked off her wellies, dried Whisky's tummy and legs and had just started on the dreaded sprouts when she looked up and saw Raff, his dark Celtic looks and black coat contrasting with the blindingly-white carpet covering the ground. His long legs moved panther-like through the deep snow. His eyes found hers and she was subjected to that intense stare that always turned her legs to jelly.

She saw him break off the gaze and look over to his left towards the driveway. A second later, she heard the crunch of tyres on snow and the drone of Em's large and ancient Land Rover. She used it to transport her sculpture commissions and it was possibly on its last legs but in these conditions, it was a good work horse and definitely more reliable than James' positively sporty Mercedes AMG-GT, which Em swore he bought as a belated male menopause trophy. His earlier car had been crushed in an incident which he still credited as the most extreme method possible to get Em to marry him.

Both Raff and Bran went over to help everyone with the boxes and bags from the car and Whisky went over to hinder. Many boxes later, they were all sitting round the big scrubbed pine table in the kitchen, drinking hot steaming coffee.

'So' said Raff eventually, 'what were the roads like through the village?'

'Pretty bad' replied James. 'Meg was holding on to the door handle for dear life on the way here.' Meg threw him an embarrassed look.

'To be fair' said Em, 'Meg always hangs on to the door handles when I'm driving. Whatever the weather.'

'I can't deny it' said Meg quietly with a smile.

'Thomas couldn't even back his car out of the driveway.' James said.

'To be fair once more, Thomas has difficulty backing out of his drive on a lovely summer's day' added Em.

'No, he's not the best of drivers' reflected Sadie, then 'Where was he trying to go in this weather?'

'We saw him walking on the way back from collecting Fran and Col's children from their next door neighbour' said Em 'Col hadn't wanted to take them in these conditions to collect their mother and had left them early this morning but the neighbour had promised to help out at the old folk's home. Then what with some of the carers not being able to get into the village… She had rung Thomas as she couldn't get hold of Col, to see if he could help out. So he walked to the other end of the village to collect them. They loved it of course, throwing snowballs at each other. Apparently, Col had said he'd be back by 12 noon as the journey was normally only an hour each way, though he said he might be a little later if his old van didn't behave itself in this weather.'

They all looked across at the clock hung at one end of the kitchen. Two thirty-five p.m. It would be getting dark in just over an hour. They took a sip of their coffee, each lost in their own thoughts.

Chapter 7

Everyone was keeping busy. Em had made some of her spiced, mulled wine. She may have been hopeless at cooking but she was a whizz when it came to alcohol.

James had set all the games out in the sitting room where they would be going after their dinner – although no one felt particularly hungry yet. He had found Sadie's old Scrabble board which they occasionally all played on at weekends.

'I'm sure there are a few tiles missing on this, that must be why you keep beating me.' Em looked at James innocently.

'Oh that's why is it? What's the tally now? Sadie, then Raff, then me – then you trailing behind I believe?' he replied.

'I think the beginning of your lucky streak was when the tiles went missing!' said Em with a sniff.

There was a new Trivial Pursuit game that Em had brought. She had bought it to replace the old one which was so old she knew all the answers so it was no fun anymore. She was worried that, with the new one, she wouldn't know *any* of the answers, especially the music ones where her idea of modern music ended with The Who and The Small Faces - and was starting to regret her purchase.

Meg was in the kitchen, red-faced from hovering over the Aga. She was working alongside Sadie, who suggested they go and throw themselves in the snow to cool off. Meg wasn't sure if she was joking but it didn't sound like a bad idea to her.

A gingerbread Bundt cake had just come out of the oven and was on the cooling rack while a salmon and asparagus tart and a veggie broccoli and mushroom one, went in to replace them.

Sadie's phone rang. Thomas again.

'Have you heard anything yet?' he asked once more. I still can't get hold of Col on the phone. I've rung the police station and they haven't had any reports of accidents but they did say that Winterfell police have put a 'Road Closed' sign over the road from there to Brytherstone across the hills as the drifts are too dangerous to attempt to drive through.

'I'm just hoping his battery is dead and that's why there is no answer' said Sadie. ' Did their neighbour find Fran's mother's phone number? Perhaps they've stayed there and the network is down?' Sadie crossed her fingers in a reflex action as she said this.

'No, Mrs Harrison says she only has Col's mobile number, he didn't leave any other one, obviously thinking he'd be back by now. You know what he's like, so laid back. Too laid back if we're honest. Although I suppose if we rang and they weren't there, that would worry Fran's mother too and she hasn't been in the best of health.'

'Which reminds me' Sadie butted in, 'is Joanna okay now? Can she manage with the children?'

'She didn't look too clever earlier but the children's arrival seems to have bucked her up. She's been entertaining them and they're now watching DVDs. Apparently they're not allowed to watch much TV at home - hippie ethics I suppose – so there was a scramble for which film to watch. Lucy and Izzy wanted Cinderella and Jack wanted Spiderman. Jack is now watching Cinderella, reluctantly, along with his sisters.'

'You know they can come up here if need be?' said Sadie.

'It might be best if I keep them here for now. They're happy – and we're happy looking after them. We're just a little worried about their parents. Let me know if you hear anything won't you?'

'Will do Thomas – and you'll do the same?'

She looked up to see Em, James and Meg all looking at her silently.

She tried to concentrate on cutting stars and hearts out of the top of mince pies, ready to go into the oven but she found her mind wandering. Raff had gone to check on his log cabin and seemed to be taking a long time. She needed to talk to him. Abandoning the mince pies, she got kitted out and tramped across the gypsy caravan clearing and over the field path to Raff's cabin which stood at the top end of Mab's Wood.

Just before she opened the front door, she heard a noise from his driveway at the other side of the cabin. Was he getting more logs for the fire from his wood store? When she went to investigate she was confronted by Raff, shovel in hands, digging the snow away from the garage/barn door where it had piled up, making it impossible to open the doors.

'Why are you doing that?' asked Sadie hesitantly 'you're not going out are you?'

Raff gave her a steady look, which answered her question.

'If I have to, yes. This is just if we haven't heard anything about Col and Fran in the next half hour. I don't think we should leave it any later than that as temperatures will start plummeting soon.'

'But then I'll worry about you too as well as them – and I love you - and this weather isn't safe for you to drive in…'

Sadie hated the selfish way that had sounded to her ears as she said it. Raff leaned the shovel against the wall and put his hands on her shoulders.

'And I love you too – but we wouldn't love each other quite as much if we weren't the sort of people who would always help our friends – no matter how much it puts us out. As far as I can, I promise you I won't put myself in danger but I can't just sit around much longer without doing something. And this Land Cruiser is the best car I could be driving in these conditions.'

Sadie put her head down.

'Raff, I'm so ashamed. I just wanted to keep you safe and I put our friends' safety second. And Fran's pregnant too! If you have to go, I'll come with you.'

'Ah, now the tables are turned because I'd rather you stayed safe at home. Maybe James…?'

James would do anything to help anyone, they both knew this.

'Let's go and check first shall we? And a hot cup of tea would go down well.' Raff said as he pulled her towards him and they walked down to Acorn Cottage, their arms wrapped around each other.

As they walked in the back door, Em was on Sadie's phone.

'It's Kit' she said, handing it over. 'Kit and Annie.'

Kit and Annie? thought Sadie, They lived over the dale in Winterfell. What could they want? Her and Raff had become quite friendly with them over the past few months after attending a solstice festival at the Winterfell Stone- an ancient standing stone on Kit's land. They had met for drinks in the pub a couple of times since but this couldn't just be a friendly Christmas Eve greeting could it?

'Sadie, it's Kit. Annie says Hi' he rushed on before she could return the greeting. 'I'm sorry to phone but, apart from the pub which I've just rung and they don't seem to know anything – you're the only people we know in Brytherstone. It's about Col and Fran.'

Sadie's heart dropped like a stone. Her face must have registered her feelings as all the occupants of the kitchen stared at her, waiting for her next words. She turned the speakerphone on so they could all hear.

'What's happened?' she managed to say. 'We've been so worried about them.'

'Well that's just it. We don't know.'

'Start at the beginning Kit' Sadie could hear Annie's calm voice from next to him.

'Earlier on today, we had to rescue Col when his van broke down. He said it wasn't the snow, it was always doing it. He broke down right on the top ridge of the hill that leads into Winterfell past our house at Hunter's Lodge. I saw him when I was walking the dogs so he and I, plus Lennie from the garage, ran it down slowly, using the handbrake, to the top of my driveway. Annie took Col in for some breakfast while Lennie had a look at the van. He said he could fix it in a couple of hours so Col phoned his wife and told her he would be late. She told him that the road conditions between Haverham and Winterfell were terrible but she'd been ringing the railway stations and luckily, of the two train routes that were still running today, the route to Winterfell was one of them. The *last* one as it happened, as they stopped running then.' He took a breath.

Kit was a respected professor of archaeology and a popular lecturer and he would be annoyed at himself for not being able to articulate his story properly. He was obviously as worried as they were.

'So' he went on 'I took him down to the station where he picked Fran up. She didn't look too good; she was as white as the snow. Whether it was the worry or the …you know she's pregnant? Yes, of course you do. Anyway, they stayed here while the van was ready. He kept trying to phone his neighbour who had the children but there was no answer. Lennie brought the van back. There was no charge as he owed me some money.'

Sadie didn't believe this for a minute. Col was short of funds and Kit obviously realised this.

'The weather was getting really bad. The landlord of your pub said it's as bad there? We asked them to stay with us rather than risk going back in that old boneshaker but they were worried about their children, especially as there was no answer from their neighbour's house…'

'They're safe at the vicar's house as the neighbour had to be somewhere else.' Sadie cut in.

'That's good at least but when they set off a good while ago, I made them promise to phone me as soon as they got back and were reunited with the children. I mentally gave them extra time for seeing the kids, getting warmed up etc – but an hour ago, after phoning the Falling Stone, Annie and I went out and trekked to the top of the hill – and then to the top of the next one, where there is a clear view for a good few miles. We couldn't see the van broken down or run off the road but we couldn't see around all the bends or over the brows of hills.

Now, the police have put a 'Road Closed' sign just past Hunter's Lodge. If they're not back and they've broken down again, it must be across the Tops or between Shepherd's Hill and Brytherstone. I wanted to come out and search but Annie said…'

'No Kit, Annie's right. It's no good everyone getting stuck in this snow. Thanks for letting us know – stay there and we'll let you know when we find anything out.'

'We'd be grateful' he said before ringing off.

'Right' said Raff, 'I'm going to look for them in the Land Cruiser. Will you come with me James? I think it might need two of us.'

James looked eager.

'Of course' he said, as they knew he would.

A strangled noise came out of Em's throat and her mouth moved silently as James turned towards her. After a second or two, she swallowed loudly and said,

'Don't forget to take shovels, blankets and phones'

Always practical' he smiled, kissing her cheek as Sadie and Em's eyes met.

'I've got shovels and blankets back at the cabin' said Raff, already making for the door – 'and we'll take the phones but there may not be mobile reception all the time. Don't worry, we'll be back as soon as we can' and with that he was off with James following on carrying a large flask of hot coffee that Meg had handed over.

It was suddenly very still and silent.

'They'll be fine' she smiled at Em.

'Of course they will' she said quietly, her eyebrows dipping down.

'I had the conversation twenty minutes ago with Raff. The same one you really wanted to have with James. "Do you really have to go?" – and he answered exactly the same as James would have done – that they wouldn't be the men we love if they didn't try to help.'

' "A friend tells you what you want to hear; a best friend tells you the truth".' sniffed Em.

'Nietzsche?' asked Sadie.

'Marilyn Monroe' replied Em with a weak smile and they both stepped forward and hugged each other tightly as Meg wiped her eyes.

Chapter 8

On the way to the cabin, Raff had rung Seth Barraclough at the pub, as he guessed correctly that he would be there.

'Seth?' he shouted into the phone after Jez had handed it over. 'Have you got your tractor in the village? With the snow plough on?'

'Well now' replied Seth, 'it depends on what you mean by 'in' the village. It's at the bottom of my farm track, ready for me to cruise back home later on.'

Seth's farm was just past the vicarage, almost opposite the turn-off to the lane leading up to Mab's Court. The 'cruising back' would happen on a half-mile straight track, leading to the farm where he lived with his parents. Drink drive rules didn't count on private land and the tractor knew its way home on automatic pilot once he'd made his way to it from the pub.

His Christmas Eve binges were legendary as he worked hard every single day but Christmas day and Boxing Day so when he finished on Christmas Eve afternoon, that was the start of his Christmas celebrations.

Raff explained the situation in a nutshell, then said, 'If I give you one hundred pounds for interrupting your only free time, would you clear a lane up that treacherous hill out of Brytherstone, just as far as you can? James and I can follow you up to the top then so there's less chance of us getting stuck? I know it's a lot to ask.'

'I've only had a pint so I'll be okay.' Seth replied.

' I can let you have more when I can get some cash out as we're so grateful that...'

'Nay, I don't want yer money, lad! Tell yer what then. You pay my bar tab at the pub for tonight's drinking and we'll call it quits. Give me five minutes to get there' he said then he was off before Raff could thank him again.

Everyone pulled together in a crisis round here. It was one of the things that Raff most loved about the place. Seth refusing money even when he wasn't that well off after this year's bad harvest, was a case in point. Raff had a very uncharitable feeling that it might have been cheaper to give him the hundred pounds than pay his bar bill before dismissing it as unworthy.

After an agonisingly slow journey down the lane in increasingly heavy snowfall, they reached the end just in time to see Seth back his tractor off the track and onto the main through road. With a swift salute as he passed them, he set off at a steady pace – the only pace the tractor was capable of – and Raff could see the snow being pushed to the left of the road to Winterfell.

'I'm going to keep a look out from here on' said James, putting his window down and when a flurry of snow flew in to engulf him, he hurriedly shut it again.

'I'll manage through the windows with the headlights. You just concentrate on driving' he advised Raff. Indeed, he needed every ounce of concentration he could muster to keep the car in a straight line, to avoid veering off into the cleared ridge of snow left in the tractor's wake.

Just before they reached the crest of the first hill, Raff could feel the wheels stop turning beneath him, losing their grip on the snow and locking into a skid. The received wisdom in these cases was not to use your brakes and just steer into the direction of the skid but as they were sliding backwards down a very steep incline, Raff pulled the handbrake on as gently as he could.

The car slewed sideways and after a few moments, ended up almost pointing back down the way they had come. James and Raff looked silently at each other before James turned to look out of the back window.

'Seth's reached the top of the hill. It looks like he's waiting there, unless he can't go any further.'

Raff tried to turn the car round, inch by inch but it only succeeded in making the car slide further back down the hill.

'It's freezing over. The wheels can't get a grip. I can't drive through the snow at the side as it's too thick and I risk getting stuck. I know,' Raff said, turning his head round to look out of the back window, 'I'll try reversing up.'

Putting it into reverse, he slowly pulled away on the icy surface and without increasing his speed, kept a steady pace until he'd reversed almost to where Seth was.

'What's Seth doing?' he asked James as he watched the tractor dancing on top of the hill. James watched for a few seconds.

'Ah, I think he's clearing a space for you to turn round in, so you're facing the right direction going down the hill on the other side.'

'Good old Seth' breathed Raff 'He'll be going back home now but this is the steepest hill to negotiate, although I'm not looking forward to the next part with the sheer drop over the right hand side.'

'Did you have to remind me of that Raff?' James smiled.

Raff reached the top of the hill and found it quite easy to turn round on the flattened snow although the last quarter turn was involuntary. He looked down into the next valley. If anything, the weather seemed worse here. There was no sign of movement or lights anywhere. It was as if a white bedsheet had been dropped from on high, over the whole land. The moon shone down now but produced a suffused light on top of the snow which didn't really help the driving conditions.

Raff turned round to see Seth in the tractor, which was now behind them – and both he and James gave him another salute to say thank you. His silhouetted figure doffed the flat cap that he always wore, in reply, then waved as they set off.

'Right. We're looking for a broken down white van, in white snow.' James said despondently.

'It's okay, the rust patches will show up against all the whiteness.' Raff gave a taut smile that didn't reach his eyes.

'What was he thinking, trying this journey in that van?' said James, his brow furrowed.

'It wasn't this bad when he set off though – and he loves his family, so he probably just wanted them all to be together for Christmas.'

'Let's pray that comes true' said James as Raff looked sideways at him. James was always upbeat – but he supposed that this situation would play havoc with anyone's joie de vivre.

As Raff put the car into gear, the snowstorm started, hitting the windscreen until there was a whiteout. The wipers couldn't keep up with it. He started forward, the blast of Seth's tractor horn as he said goodbye, puncturing the deathly silence and making them both jump.

The snow became thicker the further down the hill he went. He felt out of control, both with the car and the situation. He couldn't even see if he was drifting off the road. If he stopped, he would have to brake as the impetus of the steep downwards incline had them in its grip. He tried to keep more to the left near the rocky outcrops as at least they wouldn't leave the road.

The wind had started up again and was now howling, driving the snow into the windows so they were driving blind. The wipers made one last, juddery, slow-motion arc across the windscreen to reveal a white wall coming up to meet them.

'Raff!'

'Hold on!'

Then everything went black.

Chapter 9

Sadie had rung Thomas just after the men had left. He said he would keep the children there until he heard something definite as they had no idea of the drama that was unfolding and it was better for them to stay in blissful ignorance.

She also phoned the neighbour, Mrs Harrison and tried to stop her blaming herself for not taking the children with her. They both knew they were better off with Thomas and Joanna and it wouldn't have helped their parents' dilemma either. She asked Sadie if there was something she could do. No, nothing, was Sadie's reply.

And it was doing nothing that was getting to the women in Acorn Cottage.

Sadie went through the motions of helping Meg finish off the baking but when she nearly dropped a tray of hot mince pies, she was despatched to make everyone a cup of tea.

'Or a large whisky' said Em as a very trim Whisky twitched his ears. *Not so much of the* **large** *please!* he thought.

'*You* can have one Em, just help yourself. I daren't in case I have to go out later if Raff and James aren't back.'

'You're going out to look for a car that's out looking for another car. Good idea. I'll follow you with the Land Rover to look for all three of you.' Em raised her eyes heavenwards.

'Nobody is going anywhere' came the voice of reason from the unlikely source of Meg Flithers. 'It's no good you all going out in this. They will all be back soon and can join you both in a very large whisky.'

Em and Sadie, suitably chastened, grabbed the mugs and kettle respectively and made a pot of tea.

When there was nothing else they could do in the kitchen, having baked, prepared and cleaned everything, all they seemed to be able to do was glance at the clock every few seconds. Finally, Meg could stand it no longer.

'Follow me. We're going to the sitting room to put something cheery on. Something like Elf or Deck the Halls' she said.

'Yes, or The Day After Tomorrow – or Whiteout?' offered Em.

'Honestly Em, I'll go and choose something myself' and Meg went through after folding her apron neatly over a chair. Sadie and Em looked at each other.

'We ought to try and be upbeat' Sadie said.

'Even if time is ticking on'

'Doesn't help Em. At all.'

'No, I suppose not. Okay then, I'll beat you at a game of Trivial Pursuit.'

'Remember you brought a new, untried version up.'

'Oh yes' said Em, 'Well in that case *you* can beat *me* at a game of Trivial Pursuit.'

They trailed through to the room where the cheery glow of the woodburner failed to cheer any of them. They set the board and cards out on the coffee table, more for something to do rather than from any expectation of playing the game. Meg was flicking through the channels.

'Oh, It's a Wonderful Life is on.' She turned to them.

'No!' chorused Sadie and Em. They were trying to avoid weeping, not actively encourage it.

Whisky and Bran trotted in after them and sat looking at everyone. Whisky wasn't the most empathetic of dogs but even he could tell something was amiss. Bran, being a Border Collie and one of the most intelligent of dogs, had been unsettled for a while now, which Sadie was reading too much into.

'What colour?' said Em, holding up the blue and orange segments.

'Green' replied Sadie distractedly, which Em let pass without comment.

'Christmas with the Kranks is on?' said Meg, TV remote in hand.

'Put that on then Meg if you want to.'

'But do *you* want it on Em?'

'Meg, anything except the news and most definitely NOT the weather forecast.'

'Okay' said Meg quietly and put Christmas with the Kranks on, due to be relegated to background noise anyway. 'Yellow for me'

'Yellow. Alright' said Em and set the pieces on the board as the wooden clock on the mantelpiece ticked the seconds by.

Chapter 10

Total silence. Blackness - where before there was only white.

They were enclosed front, sides and above and the weight of the snow pressed on them.

Raff felt, rather than saw, James turn in his seat and then utter a sound which came out on a long exhalation of juddering breath.

'Raff' his voice sounded echoey, 'we're clear behind.'

Raff looked round and could see a change in the blackness. The lighter shade of a heavy night sky.

'Thank god. Let's just crawl over the seats and get out of the back door. We can get the shovels out and try and dig ourselves out of this lot.' His voice sounded both relieved and hopeful. 'You go first James; I'll wait here until you're out.'

Just at that moment, something disturbed the silence. Everything was muffled tonight, nothing seemed real – except the gloriously recognisable chug-chug of an old tractor.

'Seth?' said James from his position halfway over the seat.

The noise became louder. Raff didn't know why Seth was still here, neither did he care. He just couldn't remember when he had been as glad to hear such an unmelodious sound.

James was in the back and opening the door. Seth jumped down from the tractor, leaving its engine running and poked his head in the open door, addressing Raff.

'What was tha up to lad? Di'nt tha hear me sound t'horn? Ah were going to clear snow in front of you but you'd set off!'

'Seth, you wonderfully stubborn person, I only asked you to clear to the top of the hill. I thought you were letting us know you were going back home. We waved. You waved back.' Raff finished lamely.

'Ah weren't waving lad – Ah were signalling for thee to stop. Did'st tha think I'd leave you both in this lot. The Blakemores too?

Tha daft 'aporth. And what was tha doing driving off into t'snow drift?'

'I can assure you it wasn't intentional Seth.' Raff grinned with relief - at the solid Yorkshire tones of Seth's admonishments more than anything.

'Do you think you can get us out' asked James.

Seth reached up for a rope from the tractor and tied it onto the Land Cruiser's tow bar.

'We'll have a bloody good go! Right lad, easy does it.' Seth said, climbing back into the tractor and the snow around the car collapsed as it slowly inched out.

*

Back on the road again, they were now following Seth. Raff felt slightly more in control and had instructions from Seth 'not to go gadding off again'. The snow was still filling the sky but they had negotiated their way to the bottom of the hill and were now on their way up the next one. It was a meandering, tortuous hill with bends that they both had trouble negotiating. However, Raff's state of mind had changed because he had a definite feeling that they would find Fran and Col soon.

He hoped so as, after this hill, they would reach 'The Tops' a notorious open area on the very highest point, which was often made impassable in snow and high winds, even in much better conditions than these. If they had broken down there, they would have no shelter from the elements.

They had nearly reached the crest of the hill and James was peering through the windscreen, his eyes searching as Raff concentrated on keeping the car on the road. There was no longer a steep drop over the right-hand side now as the landscape there had gradually given way to a wooded plateau, which was the one thing he recognised in this alien landscape he was driving through. The trees which on a night stood out, the deepest black against an already dark sky, were now almost indistinguishable from everything else as their white tops just melted into the snow-sky.

Just then, there was a shout from James and he reached across to lean heavily on the horn. Seth was already slowing and pulled off to the right, Raff following him. There, in a lay-by next to the wood, was a battered old white van.

Even better, beside it, alerted by the sound of Seth's tractor, was the unmistakable figure of Col, waving his arms frantically with his wild hair covered by snowflakes.

Chapter 11

'Raff! Seth! …and James!' he shouted out.

The glee on his face went some way to give them hope that Fran was unharmed too. Col's next words though, made them think again.

'We, erm, had a little incident. It's Fran.' He nodded towards the van.

'Is she okay? Is she hurt?'

'She will be much better when we can reach home. How are the kids? Do they know we're okay?'

'You can tell them yourself when you see them Col, it won't be long now' said James kindly, while keeping his fingers crossed that was true as they still had the arduous journey back to endure.

As they walked across, Col started explaining in a torrent of words.

'The van was alright; it didn't break down again. Well, not until we'd been running it for warmth anyway – and I think it's probably just run out of fuel now. I had to pull off the road suddenly you see and after running it while it was stationary for a while, it stopped and wouldn't start again.'

'Mobile phone?' asked Raff simply.

'Nothing. No reception. Walked to the top and then through the woods and out the other side. Nothing. Didn't want to leave her for too long or I'd have attempted to walk somewhere but we're about as far from civilisation here as is possible and I couldn't see any lights from farms. Probably obscured by the blizzard.

'Flipping 'eck!' came the surprised tones of Seth as he dragged the van door open and then 'Well, I'll go t'foot of our stairs!'

Intrigued now, they all went over and peered in. There, snuggled up under the van's total supply of blankets and coats, were Fran and her extremely new-born baby.

*

Sadie's phone went off on the Trivial Pursuit board. They were in the middle of a game that no one had been able to concentrate on. Sadie was trying to answer a complex question about camera aperture speeds, which she couldn't focus on…so to speak.

'Yes! Raff! Are you alright?'

There was just white noise. Every damn thing was white tonight, thought Sadie.

'I can't hear you!' she shouted. Em was leaning forward nervously.

The phone died. They all sat there, unable to say a word or decide whether the call meant bad news or good news when it rang again.

'Raff!' Sadie almost screeching with fear.

Then she went quiet and some seconds later, replaced the phone on the table. She looked at Em.

'He said ' Everyone okay. On way home."
and the two strong, unemotional women both burst into tears, hugging each other then opening their arms to let Meg join them too.

*

Sadie made the decision to bring the children up to the cottage so that they could greet their parents. If Raff called at the vicarage first, they would direct him up here. Em drove the Land Rover down steadily as it was like a temperamental horse that would perform for no one but its owner.

'Come on you horrible lot' Em shouted at the amused and blatantly unconcerned children, who knew her well. 'We're taking you up to Acorn Cottage to see your mum and dad. They'll be arriving later'

Lucy, Izzy and Jack rushed around excitedly, packing their animal-shaped rucksacks up again, including a favourite cuddly toy, a pair of pyjamas and an extra top and underwear each which Thomas, in one of his rare moments of clarity, had insisted they pack. They treated Thomas and Joanna in a very easy manner and you could tell they had enjoyed themselves at the vicarage.

Sadie watched Joanna helping them, her cheeks flushed and a big smile on her face. As soon as the children were getting their wellies on in the hallway, Sadie whispered to Thomas,

'How is she?'

His eyes wandered fondly over the neat figure of his wife, her long light brown hair hanging forward as she helped push Jack's boots on.

'She seems fine now but...' the worry sprang to his eyes 'there's something wrong. I just feel there is. She has always confided in me so I just have to keep faith that she would do so if anything was really wrong.'

He smiled weakly and Sadie reached out to squeeze his arm.

Without being asked, the children all gave a hug to Joanna and then came to give Thomas one too. He blushed and shuffled a bit but looked very pleased all the same.

'Thank you for having them, both of you' said Em, 'They seem to have had a lovely time.'

'We have too,' said Joanna 'the noise has brought the vicarage to life.'

'They weren't *too* noisy though' smiled Thomas. 'We'd look after them again, wouldn't we Joanna?'

His wife smiled and nodded as she held the door open, waving them off. Sadie turned round.

'Are you sure we can't persuade you to come for dinner tomorrow?' she asked.

'And you haven't been too well' Thomas added as though she needed reminding.

'I'm positive but thank you all the same' replied Joanna. 'I have all the food in now and with the roads as they are at the moment, I'd feel safer staying inside.'

'Are you questioning my driving abilities again dear?' beamed Thomas before he went to help strap the children in the seats.

Joanna leant in towards Sadie and whispered,

'And I'd like it to be just the two of us when I give Thomas his Christmas present.'

Out of anyone else's mouth, that might have elicited a different - and slightly lewd – response but Sadie looked into Joanna's warm grey eyes, hesitated for a moment, then smiled. She left her with a kiss on the cheek and a hug.

'Get in touch on Christmas day' she urged as Joanna nodded.

Chapter 12

'Alright you three'

Em addressed Lucy, Izzy and Jack who were looking around them in awe at all the twinkling lights and sumptuous decorations.

'Meg is going to arrange something to keep us occupied until everyone else gets here.'

Em pretended she wasn't a 'children-person' but her actions had always given the lie to her words. Somehow, children always gravitated towards her. Sadie knew she had felt the same pull when she was young and used to come and stay with her. However much her aunt tried to deny it – Em was fun!

'I've got some very plain-looking cookie baubles that need jazzing up before they can be hung on the Christmas tree. I've got red, blue and green icing. Who fancies a go?'

Meg held the icing tubes out to them as they each grabbed a colour in readiness.

'Where's my icing?' sulked Em.

'You can all share' laughed Meg.

The reason they were all trying to distract themselves was because there was no sign or word of Raff and the rest. As Sadie knew it was no good trying to get in touch again- they would phone her if they could get reception – the only thing to do was just wait.

After fifteen minutes and a few choruses of 'Frosty the Snowman' from Lucy and Izzy. All the baubles were done and being hung on the tree in the dining room. When they all came back in, looking a bit lost now, Em and her exchanged meaningful glances.

'I know' said Sadie in the manner of a Blue Peter presenter, 'I have some leftover felt in my study, would you each like to make a present for your mum and dad, for when they get here?'

'Oh yes! I'm going to make an angel' said Lucy.

'And I'll make a snowman' Izzy shouted.

'And I'm going to make Rudolph' said Jack, the youngest, then he started singing Rudolph the red-nosed reindeer very loudly.

Sadie found herself thinking how self-contained these children were. They were as happy and laid-back as their parents. All that happened was one sentence from Lucy as they came in, asking if their parents were here yet, then just an exchange of glances between the three of them before they carried on as normal. It was only when there was a lull that their brows furrowed, hence keeping them busy with no time to think. She couldn't help thinking that she would like such lovely children someday.

As she back walked into the kitchen, Em had started singing 'Rudolph' too at the top of her voice. Sadie tried not to make a hasty exit even though Em's singing voice had been likened to that of Groucho Marx.

Sadie cut out the shapes for them, put the sequins, glitter, stickers and glue on the table and left them to the tender ministrations of her aunt and her adoptive aunt.

She went down the passageway and pulling her heavy woollen duffel coat on, she opened the front door.

The cold hit her. Even more than before. Of course it was later now and she had become warmed up in the lovely, cosy kitchen but it was still well below freezing and the roads would be even more treacherous than before. She shivered involuntarily.

She closed the door behind her to keep the warmth in and stood under the porch. The snow had stopped falling now but it afforded her a little shelter from the cold. She smiled as she remembered how Raff had carved this porch for her, even before she knew him well and before she admitted to herself that she was falling for him.

Raff hand-carved wood for commissions. Many of them were for churches - to renew or replace the original figured panels or pulpits that were there. Many were also in stately homes. Perhaps work on balustrades, panelling or intricate friezes. Others were one-off commissions of wooden sculptures, from eagles for the American embassy down to a gift of a beautifully carved box from a husband to his wife.

Yet for Sadie, his greatest achievement was this simple, wooden, open porch. Built in English oak, it had a rustic design. The thing that made it stand out was a sophisticated carved pediment, formed in the triangular apex of the porch. It was filled with carvings of acorns and oak leaves with a central oak tree standing proud – and the magical words 'Acorn Cottage' below it. It made her heart swell with pride every time she saw it, firstly because of her lovely forever home and also because of the wonderful man who had carved it.

She smiled, then scanned the lane far below, which was at the bottom of the front garden and the driveway on the left – and past Mab's Court. She looked for any signs of life. Everything was silent.

She raised her eyes towards the sky, which earlier had alternated between snow-filled grey, yellow or white and an angry purple. Now the snow had stopped falling and the wind had dropped, the night sky had opened up into a black velvet background hung with the brightest stars. One star shone brighter than the others and on a night like tonight – Christmas Eve – one couldn't help but be reminded of the age-old story.

She lowered her eyes and as they got used to the covered ground below her, she noticed that the white mass of snow was not completely clear. She peered towards what would have been the lawn then stepped out from the fairy lights of the porch, onto the terrace and down into the relative darkness a few feet further on.

Small animal prints had appeared, probably from the squirrels that lived in the trees bordering the garden to the right. Larger ones, possibly the fox that kept making a fleeting appearance in its search for food. As she thought this, she noticed a few bird tracks underneath the feeders hung just past the terrace. They had obviously become brave enough, since the blizzard, to venture out from shelter.

She surveyed the scene, her eyes sweeping over to her right, towards where her land carried on towards Mab's Wood from the thicket of native woodland trees nearby. The snow canopy of the trees stood out now against the black night sky, even as the moon surfaced from behind a cloud. Then she saw it. Everything became silent. The noise from inside receded into nothingness. A small deer stood there, pale against the reflected snow. It had stopped, mid-stride and was now turned towards her.

As it looked at her, their eyes met for a moment before it turned back towards the trees and across to Mab's Wood. That single, sublime moment had produced in Sadie a remarkable feeling of calm that replaced all the anxieties of earlier. She knew something had happened and felt privileged beyond belief to have felt or witnessed this. She had seen deer many times before around here – but this one had looked deep into her soul.

Sadie wasn't sure how long she stayed out there. The noise inside was still diminished, the air itself seemed warmer. She suddenly felt like she wanted to communicate all this to Em, to tell her everything was alright, without having the first idea where to start with her famously no-nonsense aunt.

As she turned to go back to the house, something made her stop. She turned and heard the chug-chug of a tractor, then a light in the distance. After a few minutes, the lights swung right into the driveway – followed by another set of lights – heading steadily up towards her.

They were home.

Chapter 13

Sadie was running alongside Raff's car as though she was re-enacting the scene from Brief Encounter. He put the window down and said,

'If you slip, you'll disappear under the wheels and into the snow, not to be found again until the thaw' which dispelled any romantic scenarios straight away.

Nevertheless, as soon as he got out, she flung herself at him and wrapped her legs round him, nearly pulling him over. He grabbed her in a bear hug, resting his head against hers before pulling away.

'There was only one place I could get a signal…' he started to explain.

'I don't care. Not anymore. I'm just so glad you're home.'

Realising she was ignoring the others, she hugged them all, stepping back in shock when she came to Fran.

'Shh!' Col smiled as he put a finger to his lips. 'It's a surprise for the kids.'

'You can say that again' squeaked Sadie, 'it's a surprise for us all!'

As they went up to the French doors outside the kitchen, they could hear the cheerful strains of Sadie's silly Christmas CD playing loudly. Singing along at the top of their voices were all three children, Meg – and what sounded like a Canada goose in the mating season, which could only be Em.

James banged on the door loudly on purpose to make them all look up and opened it as Em ran up to him. She paused, looking embarrassed but then flung her arms round him.

'Oh, what the hell' she said, kissing him, 'and don't you ever do your Dan Dare bit again!'

Next through were Col and Fran. The children shouted in excitement and ran full pelt towards them until Lucy stopped short. Izzy ran into the back of her and Jack peered round them both, a little puzzled.

'A baby!' the girls yelled. 'You've had the baby!'

Jack came shyly up to the little bundle, lying peacefully in its mother's arms and he stroked its cheek softly.

'Is it a boy?' he whispered.

'It is' his mother smiled at him.

Jack held up the white figure of a deer with a shiny red sequin for a nose.

'It's Rudolph. I made it for you but the baby can have it now.'

'Thank you Jack' smiled Fran 'You don't know just how perfect that is for him' and she held him close with her other arm, while exchanging a knowing glance with her husband.

'Why? Are you going to call him Rudolph? asked Jack, obviously thinking it was a good idea by the look on his face.

'Shall we let your mum and your new brother get warm in front of the fire first?' suggested Sadie and led Fran over to the comfy chair near the Aga.

'And your dad?' offered Col as Sadie smiled, indicating another chair.

Lucy and Izzy held up the angel and the snowman to give to the baby too – and Fran suggested they could all make it into a Christmas mobile to hang from the ceiling for their brother to see as it twirled round.

Seth had gone across and pressed a pound coin into the tiny baby's hand.

'Don't reckon it's silver no more, but it'll still mek sure he has a good start in life.'

He then handed the coin to Col and went over to join Raff at the far side of the kitchen. He took his well-worn flat hat off and his sandy-coloured hair stood up on end as he tried in vain to smooth it down. Two minutes later they both had one elbow on the worktop while the other one was helping to lift a large glass of whisky to their mouths.

The dogs had stopped charging about on the floor with all the excitement and had both sprawled themselves over Raff's feet as their own, practical way of stopping him going out again.

'Here's to you Seth' said Raff, holding his glass up.

'Hear hear' said James from across the kitchen.

'Here's to *all* of you' countered Em. 'We're very proud of you all.'

Col took the glass that James offered him and addressed the men.

'We want to say how very grateful we are that you were brave enough to come looking for us. I don't know what would have happened if you hadn't, as we didn't realise the road was closed off. We kept hoping to see a gritter or a snow plough but there was just nothing.

I don't think we've ever been as pleased to see anyone in our lives as we were to see you three – and I don't know how we can ever thank you enough'

'I echo every word Col said – and thank you from this little one especially.' Fran smiled down at the infant feeding happily in her arms.

'We were more than happy to help' replied James.

'I have to say' said Raff, 'that Seth is the hero of the hour. I dragged him away from his Christmas Eve booze-up at the 'Stone' and he went above and beyond what I asked him to do. In fact, after I ran into a snow drift, I'll go as far as to say we might not have reached your van without him. He's even cleared the snow to one side of the lane and Acorn Cottage driveway. So, here's to Seth!'

'To Seth' they all shouted and gave him three cheers.

'Aw, go on with yer' said Seth with his already ruddy cheeks getting redder and looking embarrassed and pleased at the same time.

He couldn't be persuaded to stay for a bite to eat before he made his way back to the pub but Meg shoved a steak pasty into his hand as he went – and it was all eaten by the time he started the tractor up. Tucked behind the seat was a bottle of fifteen year old Scotch reserve from James. The sound of the engine pierced the quiet night air. There was a little deputation, braving the cold, waving like crazy as the tractor trundled down the driveway, taking Seth to resume his Christmas Eve 'session'.

*

'How on earth did you stay so calm' Sadie said. She looked at the Earth Mother that was Fran, looking as though she had done nothing more that day than read a good book.

They were still sitting round the table after eating warm salmon quiche, maple ham and egg quiche and a mushroom tart for the vegetarian Blakemore family. Potato salad, leaf salad and crisps accompanied them. That was followed by iced gingerbread Bundt cake with cream or custard to follow. They now had mugs of hot chocolate in front of them with mini-mallows on the top for the children and brandy cream for the adults.

'You know what Fran's previous job was, don't you?' replied Col, frowning as he tried to remember if they'd mentioned it. Fran smiled at him.

'I was a Sister-in-charge at Settle general hospital – and I did three years midwifery. That's why I wouldn't let you call the doctor out tonight. It was a straightforward birth - even if the circumstances were somewhat unusual – and everything went well. This young man is feeding well too, so everything is as it should be.'

'We had no idea of your background before you moved here' said Em, 'we just thought you were one of those eminently capable women who could give birth miles from anywhere in the middle of a blizzard, whilst spinning a plate on your big toe and reciting 'Paradise Lost' in Spanish.'

Fran laughed as Col said seriously, 'She could probably recite it in French.'

'Col!' his wife said, 'It's nice that you think that but although I'm fluent in French, I definitely don't know 'Paradise Lost' off by heart.'

'But if you did…' he smiled at her fondly.

Sadie had phoned Joanna and Thomas, then Kit and Annie and had gone through the whole story twice to cries of amazement.

Meg and Em cleared the mugs off the table as Sadie set the children to making their mobile. They now resumed the 'name-game'.

'Well, if you're not calling him Rudolph, what about Blitzen?' asked Jack.

'No, call him Santa' said Izzy.

'Or Frosty?' added Lucy.

The adults now joined in…and Em.

'Noel?' suggested Meg.

'What about Blizzard as he was born in one?' said James.

'That sounds like another of Santa's reindeers. How about Bambi?' Raff grinned.

'Yes!' the girls chorused 'Bambi!'

'I know' Em joined in, 'you could call him Jesus?'

'Em!' Meg scolded Em sternly.

'You still don't take any winding up Meg' laughed Em.

'Spiderman!' shouted Jack.

His parents laughed and Col said,

'Me and your mum are going to have a little think about it tonight, to see what suits him – and then, when you come down for breakfast in the morning, we'll let you all know.

The young Blakemores cheered and jiggled in their chairs before getting down to some serious Christmas mobile-making for their unnamed brother.

Chapter 14

Christmas Day

Sadie had asked Fran and her family to stay overnight. Well, she'd actually told them, not asked. Sadie wondered if she was turning into Em. She supposed that seeing her at least four times a week was bound to have some sort of adverse effect on her. Em and James were already staying in one of the guest doubles, while Meg had a comfy single above Sadie's study, overlooking the front.

She had put Fran, Col and Baby Blakemore in the room that was ready for Ali and George. The three children shared the room put aside for Ali's two boys. They had pushed the twin beds together - they were the type that made into a double bed – and even amidst all the excitement of Christmas and having a new baby brother, they were out like a light when Sadie popped her head round the door, twenty minutes later.

She had made sure the room was toasty warm for the baby as he was sleeping in a large basket with handles, that Sadie had bought to put a display of herbs in but hadn't yet used. They had lined it well but she had a feeling that he wouldn't be moving far away from his mum's arms through the night. From her bedroom, Sadie had heard him give a little hungry cry just once but after that, she had slept soundly, wrapped in Raff's arms.

He had put his fingers to his lips this morning when she caught him getting dressed at an ungodly hour. He had offered to take Col to fetch the sack of the children's presents from their cottage in the village – and also the nut roast from the fridge which was the only reason they could persuade them all to stay for Christmas dinner. Col had to bring the suitcase, already packed for Fran's stay in hospital, before their youngest son had decided to put in an early appearance. It had tiny baby clothes in, cream etc – and the most important thing of all - nappies. They had been using a small sample pack which Fran had tucked into the van's glove compartment and forgotten about till last night.

The children had already packed overnight things in their backpacks yesterday when Thomas had collected them. Col just needed to pick up a change of clothes for him and Fran, toothbrushes and the carry cot.

Their small, rented cottage was impossible to keep warm – Fran had told Sadie this the night before, saying the shop unit at Mab's Court was warmer than their sitting room. The landlady wouldn't make any improvements as she was selling it in the Spring, which was why they all had to be out. Sadie had looked at Meg's face at the time and just knew she was going to offer to let them stay at her little cottage but it was hardly any bigger than theirs, which they had already outgrown.

If the worst came to the worst and they hadn't found somewhere else in three months' time, then Sadie would let them stay at Acorn Cottage until they found a new place.

Now, Sadie crept downstairs. She couldn't get back to sleep anyway after Raff had gone and she had a load of things to do. She filled the kettle up for her 'wake up' coffee and had just pulled her list out from behind the jug on the dresser when she heard Raff's car, crunching on the snow.

He and Col came in after taking their snow-covered boots off and Col took the sack through to the sitting room to put the presents under the smaller tree there, leaving a dish with the nut roast on the table. Sadie transferred it to the fridge and frowned. Raff was very quiet. Was he trying not to disturb the baby?

He went to make the fires up in the sitting room and the dining room and then came back to put some more wood on the Aga. When Sadie asked him if he wanted a coffee, he didn't seem to hear. She stopped what she was doing.

'Raff' she said quietly.

He seemed to come to and looked across at her, his smile dispelling any fears.

'What were the roads like?' she asked him.

'Still bad. It's not thawing at all. No more snow – or maybe just a covering. You only have to be out in it for a few minutes before you can't feel your nose.' He leant over and gave her a kiss.

'Happy Christmas morning, my love' he whispered.

'Oh – and a very happy Christmas morning to you Raff. Our first together.' She smiled, relaxing now.

'But not our last by any means' he said as their eyes met. He reluctantly pulled his gaze away.

'I'll be back to be your servant for the day soon but first I'm going to check on my cabin. I'll take those two reprobates, snuggling in their blankets and pretending they're not here.'

He looked across at the dogs, calling them. Bran put his head up, shook his ears, then obediently trotted over to Raff. Whisky carried on pretending he wasn't there.

'Whisky! You're getting worse' laughed Sadie. 'You're a fair weather dog. A bit of snow won't hurt you.'

How do you know? thought Whisky, *Have you ever put your delicate little paws onto what you thought was solid ground and seen them disappear, leaving your fluffy little tum freezing cold too? I thought not and I rest my case.*

'Did you hear me Whisky?' said Sadie, next to his ear.

I've suddenly gone deaf, thought Whisky, *It's the cold – it affects my ears. Best stay right where I am, don't you think?*

Raff grinned at Sadie who said they weren't going to win and she'd just let him out of the back door later.

The light was trying to break through the windows now, reflecting white from the snow – but the insides of the rooms were still dark. Sadie had turned all the corner lamps on in the farmhouse kitchen and the lights over the table and the Aga too. Now she went round switching on all the many lamps that were dotted around the place. She felt they had more ambience than an all-encompassing overhead light.

The hallstand lamp was already on and now she went into the sitting room. There was a large bay window with a cushioned window seat of midnight blue velvet, which echoed the settee and chairs in there. The cream carpet might have been a mistake, acknowledge Sadie, as she thought of the footfall today. Adults, children and dogs. It did look nice though, contrasting against the suite.

She switched the corner lamps on and also a vintage standard lamp behind her winter reading chair. She switched the golden fairy lights on that spiralled round the smaller Christmas tree. This one, in the corner past where the woodburner was now burning brightly, was dressed tastefully in cream and gold.

Hanging from the mantelpiece was a swag of fir branches tied together and decorated with pine cones, holly berries and gold baubles. Along the top were a few gold candles in jars, sparkling with glitter. On the coffee table, next to an arrangement of gold-sprayed cones in a bowl, were two large church candles.

Sadie switched off the redundant overhead light and went back down the hall, turning right into the dining room, where they would eat later. The fire was flickering nicely in the dog-grate and Raff had put the brass fire-guard securely round it for now.

In the right-hand corner stood the floor to ceiling real Christmas tree that Sadie had dreamed of having there, ever since she moved in. It was such a perfect 'Christmas house' that she couldn't help it.

In contrast to the sitting room tree, this one was traditionally decorated in red and green with all the usual culprits hanging from it. The nutcracker prince, rocking horses, robins, angels, icicles and candy canes – with lots of shiny red baubles and a red sparkly chain wound around it. She turned on the switch for the fairy lights, which brought the whole tree to life.

Arrangements of red berry lights were cascading from the two ambient lights which hung over the table, filtering the light into a misty red. These echoed the red berries in glass containers on the table runner, each with an artificial tea light which would give out a rosy glow.

Sadie checked the crystal wine glasses, adding three glass tumblers from the dresser cupboard for the children. She picked up the felt tip pen she had left next to a pile of place markers. She had cut out snowmen from white card and decorated them. They each held a banner above their heads and now, Sadie wrote everyone's name on them. She put them in their places, along with the shiny red and green Christmas crackers, next to each place setting.

Finally, she switched on the lamp on the dresser and the lamp on the small console table next to the French windows, which also held the wine for the meal. She took one last, satisfied look at it – her heart giving a little jump of glee- then went back into the kitchen for a coffee.

After clearing the table of her mug from earlier and washing it under the tap, she put the electric kettle on again to boil quickly as there was only her downstairs at the moment. Looking over to the Aga, she saw the lights weren't on and went to switch them on but nothing happened. Disappointed but realising it would probably be a fuse, she resolved to ask Raff to change it when he came back, as part of his 'servant' duties for the day.

She looked out of the window. There were a few gentle flakes making their way down to the ground. She hadn't checked the weather forecast but the sky, although still heavy, didn't look as ominous as yesterday.

A watched kettle never boils. This is true but as Sadie put her finger tentatively on it, she realised it was stone cold. With an awful realisation, she turned round and saw there was no more rosy glow from the stark-looking lamps. Yet she had just switched them all on in the dining room. It must be a main fuse that had blown in the kitchen. Of all the times for it to go. She hoped that it could be mended quickly.

Just to make sure, she walked slowly back to the dining room, where the only light that now met her, came from the fire still burning steadfastly there.

Em appeared in the room behind her and put her hand on Sadie's shoulder.

'Ah yes. I forgot to tell you about Brytherstone's famous winter power cuts, didn't I?'

Chapter 15

'Power cuts?' Sadie turned around to face her aunt. '*Famous* power cuts?'

'Yep' Em said, totally unconcerned even though there was the small matter of Christmas Day celebrations and accompanying food to stress out over.

'How long do they actually last?' Sadie asked, her voice rising an octave.

'Could be as little as ten minutes.' Em said as Sadie's shoulders relaxed a little. 'Or it could be twenty-four hours or more.' Sadie's shoulders shot up on a level with her earlobes.

'Nnnff' she grunted, her mind immediately going to the worst case scenario. She looked at Em helplessly. 'Christmas dinner?'

'It may be that it's my brain that's addled instead of yours but I rather thought you had solid fuel and log fires and a wood-fired Aga? I think you'll find that the only thing affected is the electricity, which will affect your radiators and water but – the cooking should be fine.' You won't have lights though.' Em finished.

'My fairy lights! My lamps!' wailed Sadie.

'The place is warm now so everyone currently upstairs will be warm until they get dressed and come down – and then they can keep warm in front of the fires and stove.'

'This is a disaster' Sadie groaned.

'Only if you make it so' scolded Em. 'You're a practical person girl, think practically!'

This galvanised Sadie into a different train of though and after a minute or two, she disappeared from the kitchen.

Meg came down the stairs looking bright-eyed and bushy-tailed, ready to join Sadie in the Christmas cooking marathon.

'Managed a shower before the power went off' she said 'and I heard a bath being run for the children earlier, so they should be alright.'

'Mum and dad jumped in after them too' laughed Col from halfway up the stairs. 'I gather we are having one of our power cuts. It feels like the seventies still in this village sometimes.'

James popped his head round the front door, he had come down with Em and immediately put outdoor wear on to go out.

'Have you got ten minutes to spare Col?' he said 'I can't find Raff anywhere and we need to bring in an extra supply of logs to keep us all warm.'

'Of course, I'll just get my coat and boots and meet you outside the back door.'

'And my husband thinks that this sort of thing is still left to the man of the house, which is why he hasn't asked for my help' said Em, disparagingly.

'Oh, glad you mentioned it my sweet. We'd love your help, wouldn't we Col?' replied James with an innocent smile.

Em looked at Meg.

'I'm going to keep quiet next time' she said.

'That'll be a first' grinned Meg.

'Meg Flithers! I'm not giving you your orange and a sixpence for Christmas now. You'll have to do without.' Em said, going for her coat.

Meg laughed and went into the kitchen, opening the fridge door. She took one look at the turkey before deciding she needed help to lift it out. She put the ham in the oven to bake and the pork in the smaller oven to slow-roast.

Meanwhile, Sadie had emptied two large boxes from her study and put all the candles from them on three large trays – designated for kitchen, sitting room and dining room. When she had placed these around each room, she went to the broom cupboard and pulled out a large box from the floor at the back. It contained all the twinkly fairy lights that had been strung through each tree during her summer evening housewarming party. Some were solar powered but many were battery-operated and there were several spare packets of batteries in the box.

Then she reached up to the shelf and brought a box of lanterns down. Some were battery-powered and emitted a strong light, which would be useful in the cooking areas. Others for holding candles or tea lights and she could use them instead of open candles where there were draughts from doors opening and closing – or near curtains.

Sadie hung the strings of fairy lights around both trees and over the garlands on the stairs and in the kitchen. Then, remembering the electric powered fairy lights outside, she hung the remaining strings around the porch and over the two small box bushes in tubs at either side of the doorway. She was just placing candles on the deep sill of a small window in the kitchen when she saw Raff. He came through the door carrying a large log basket overflowing with logs.

'Did you plan this power cut so that you could use your prodigious supply of candles up and say 'I told you so'?' he laughed and kissed her on her cheek.

'I *did* tell you so! You can never have too many candles. And if I'd known you were prone to power cuts round here, I'd have bought even more.' Sadie told him.

'There are no more candles to be had. You've bought everyone in a ten mile radius' Raff responded.

'It's a good job I did. It might be almost daylight but the weather makes it dark inside – and we need a warm glow at Christmas' said Sadie, having the last word. 'Did James give you that log basket? He was wondering where you were.'

'Yes he did. I was a little longer than I thought – but I'm all yours now.'

'Promises, promises' and she went off to put the lanterns in the places she had selected.

There was a sudden, thunderous rumble and the Blakemore children galumphed down the stairs, shouting out 'Merry Christmas!' Their parents followed on with the most junior member of the family.

'Merry Christmas' said Fran. 'Is it okay if the children go into the room and open their presents? We'll get no peace until they do.'

Of course' said Sadie, 'the woodburner is lit but just let me put these lanterns in then you will have more light.'

'Ohh!'

The girls stopped at the sitting room door, their eyes wide, and Jack said 'Wow!'.

'This looks wonderful' said Fran, beaming at Sadie. 'It looks even better with all the candles than it did before.'

Sadie let her eyes roam around the room. It really did, it looked much more Christmassy than before- with almost like a Victorian or even medieval feel to it – and it was almost as light as before. Maybe it was fate. Maybe this had happened so they could have a real traditional first Christmas at Acorn Cottage. She smiled at this flight of fancy but half-believed it anyway. It really was glowing with golden warmth.

She then went to help manhandle the turkey out of the fridge and into a giant baking tin.

'You've checked it will fit in the Aga, haven't you?' asked Em who was warming herself up in front of it.

Sadie stopped putting streaky bacon over it and looked uncertainly at Meg, as Meg looked uncertainly at the oven.

'I haven't *measured* it exactly' gulped Sadie.

'I mean, it's a huge oven' offered Meg, helpfully.

'It's a huge turkey' said Em, not helping one bit.

After stuffing, buttering, bacon-ing and foiling the turkey in silence, Sadie and Meg each lifted one end of the baking tray while Em held the Aga door open. They held their breath as they slid the tray in very slowly – and then let it out again collectively. There wasn't a lot of clearance on the top and sides but there was enough for it to roast well.

Three figures came charging up to them, excitedly holding out their presents to show everyone.

'I'm trying to keep them out of your way in here' laughed Fran 'but they couldn't wait to show you.'

'They're fine' smiled Sadie, admiring the carved wooden jewellery boxes for the girls with a ballerina twirling round to Swan Lake in each – and a carved wooden pirate's chest for Jack, complete with chocolate gold and silver coins.

'They're beautiful' she breathed and after a few minutes of quiet thought, she asked Meg if she could hold the fort for a little while. Meg, who would quite happily do every bit of the meal by herself as she loved every minute of it, readily agreed.

Raff came back in after leaving the last of the logs by the door.

'Right you three' he said, addressing the children now being herded back into the sitting room. 'Get your coats and wellies on and follow me.' Excitement showed on their faces as there was a scrabble for outdoor wear. Sadie quietly put hers on and went out, down the driveway to Mab's Court. Seth's snow clearing the previous night had made the way easier.

She reached the untrodden snow of the courtyard itself and brought a set of keys out of her pocket. On reaching Shelley's jewellery unit, she unlocked the door and went in. It was dark inside so she got her phone out for a little light. Everything was still set out for the Christmas Eve opening that didn't happen. Necklaces, bracelets and rings were set out on faux-velvet display cards.

Sadie reached towards the back of the display to a selection of children's bracelets. There were two that appealed to her, one, made out of daisies linked together and the other one of yellow roses both on silver bands. She pulled them down and put them in two bags. She wouldn't leave cash here but would let Shelley know what she'd taken and would pay her when the Court opened up again.

She walked to a black card at the side of the counter, filled with small silver charms.

Shelley had put a few Christmas related ones at the bottom. Sadie wasn't sure if it was Rudolph or just a stag but she picked it anyway.

Now, she just had to find where Shelley had put the stones she had been showing her a couple of weeks ago. She tried the drawers, hoping they weren't locked. Some were but the third one revealed the treasure…literally. There were bags full of large fake jewels shining through the white gauze. Their colours sparkled citrine yellow, emerald green. sapphire blue and ruby red. Perfect!

Putting everything in her pockets and writing an I.O.U to Shelley with a list of what she'd taken, she made her way back up the driveway.

She could hear the noise before she saw them. She slipped through the line of trees to the left of the driveway into the large front garden of Acorn Cottage. She stayed next to the trees, unnoticed for a minute and took in the scene.

The children were laughing, ruddy-faced with the cold, while rolling snowballs up in their mittened hands. Raff was battling valiantly against the onslaught whilst making a snowman, which had obviously started as a joint effort. He marshalled them into going back to a second snow-boulder and they rolled it up to the first, larger one. A cheer went up as they lifted it then they set themselves the task now of making the snow-head.

She smiled happily at the scene and looked behind them at Acorn Cottage itself. The snow was still thick on the roof but had slid away from the two sets of chimneys. Icicles were hanging from the windowsills and were reflecting the twinkling lights Sadie had hung up earlier. There was a thick coating of snow on the oak porch roof and from inside the house, the candlelight flickered through the windows giving the whole cottage a cosy warmth.

The next minute, a wet and scraggy ball of fluff came hurtling towards her, jumping straight up into Sadie's arms to soak her coat through and generally doing that dog-thing of greeting her as if she'd been away for a week when she'd only been away fifteen minutes, tops. Whisky had got his second wind – or found his second puppyhood.

As Bran came down to join him, Whisky flew back towards Raff and immediately jumped into the snow-head they'd just made, which made him disappear in a cloud of disintegrating snow. Bran joined him as they jumped and circled in the resulting pile of slush.

Sadie hoped it wouldn't upset the children but as they were rolling on the ground in gales of laughter, she swiftly dismissed that thought. As she passed, they had already started making another head for the snowman, with Whisky 'helping' to push it with his nose. She grinned at Raff and started to go around the house to the back door when she felt something hit her on the back of the head, snow falling over her shoulders.

She turned to see Raff pointing at the three youngsters who in turn were giggling and pointing earnestly at Raff.

'It was HIM' shouted Jack conclusively.

'I believe you Jack' Sadie said.

She raised her eyebrows at Raff and turned back. Before she had reached the side of the house, she looked back and saw Raff was standing, smoothing out the snowman's body before the snow-head was lifted on to it. She bent down and, armed, stood back up then,

Thwack- a perfect hit on the back of his head. She disappeared quickly down the side of the house, the children's laughter ringing in her ears.

Chapter 16

Most of the food was either prepared or ready cooking. Considering the catastrophe that both the power cut and being cut off from the rest of the world could have been, things were going swimmingly. Even though Sadie had been up hours, it was still early and it was now time for the Christmas breakfast. This particular breakfast was reindeer-shaped pancakes with blueberries for the eyes and a raspberry for the nose for the kids. For the adults there was eggs Benedict on muffins with smoked salmon – and pork pie for Em.

'Why pork pie?' asked Sadie.

'Tradition round here in Yorkshire. Well it was when I was growing up anyway. We were given two massive pork pies from the Winterhill estate who your grandfather worked for – and if we didn't eat it for breakfast, we'd never have got through them.'

Sadie watched as Em added a huge dollop of brown sauce to her plate.

'Besides, it's Christmas' offered Em 'If I wanted cold Chinese curry for breakfast, no one with any heart could deny me it.'

'What about those with good food sense, could they deny you it?' asked Meg.

'Mmm' said Raff to puzzled looks. 'I'm partial to leftover curry the next day myself.'

Meg had a mutinous look on her face.

'You are not having curry in any form Raff Maguire, so sit down and eat what you're given'

Raff looked suitably chastened. The usually mild-mannered Meg only became dictatorial where food was concerned.

'I didn't mean for now Meg, I'm really looking forward to this, it looks delicious.'

'I allow Em her pork pie as she is not known for her gastronomic palate – but no one else.'

'Good grief' exclaimed Em.

'Are you as shocked as I am at Meg's newly acquired bossiness?' laughed Sadie.

'No, I'm just shocked she can come up with the words 'gastronomic palate' this early in the morning'

'Eat your pork pie' said Meg, dismissively.

'Mu-um' began Jack, 'you said you'd tell us the baby's name this morning.'

This set the girls off too and they all clamoured to know what the name would be. Their parents smiled at each other and Col said,

'We haven't got a first name yet as we need to do more research but we have a middle name.'

'We've all got middle names' said Lucy 'mine's Ann'

'It is sweetheart. We would like the first name to be a special name. His middle name though will be Seth, after our tractor hero.'

Everyone turned to each other in glee over this popular choice.

'Special in what way?' asked James, picking up on the earlier comment.

'Well it's a strange story really'. Fran looked up at her husband as he told the tale. 'As you know, we were stuck at the side of a remote road last night with Fran just having given birth. There was a blizzard around us, blotting out the landscape.

We are optimists by nature and we were sure everything would work out well. However, as time went by, we were getting a little worried. We hadn't seen any other vehicles – even emergency ones – and we didn't know the road had been closed.

I felt like I ought to try and walk to find help but I also knew that if anything happened to me and I didn't make it, it would put Fran and the baby in danger too. I had almost made my mind up, against all Fran's cautions, to walk back towards Winterfell. A stupid idea in those conditions, I now realise. The baby wouldn't feed at first and Fran was trying to keep calm for his sake.

Just for a few minutes, the blizzard stopped. I got out of the van and cleared the windscreen and got back in quickly. We were both just staring bleakly out of the windscreen towards the trees when suddenly there was a movement.

A small deer appeared from the woods. It was paler than normal and - I can't explain – it just felt so surreal. It just walked round so it was directly in front of us – gazed at us with the most beautiful, intense, *knowing* eyes - then slowly wandered off into the woods again.'

'The strangest thing was' continued Fran, taking up the story, 'that when it was looking at us, neither of us said a thing. We just felt this overwhelming sense of calm. A feeling that all was right with the world – which was ridiculous, considering our situation. Nevertheless, we continued to feel the same even after the deer had gone – and even when the blizzard came back less than a minute later – worse than ever.'

'So…' said Col 'we stopped worrying. We knew that all would be well. The baby started to feed and five minutes later we saw the lights and just after, heard the noise of the tractor. The rest is history. So – we wanted to celebrate this event somehow in his name but we are still thinking how.'

In the midst of everyone exclaiming on the story with expressions of wonder, Raff noticed Sadie's silence.

'Sadie?' he said gently but everyone caught the inflection and looked across at her in silence.

'Nothing' she said. Nothing? Why did she say that? They were all looking at her. It was her turn to explain the unexplainable.

'Alright then, there is something. Something that ties the two events together. Just before you all arrived back last night I was out on the front terrace, watching for signs of your return. There had been no word for a while – which was only to be expected anyway because of the weather – but I was still worried.

As I stood there, I looked over to the trees at the edge of the land and I saw a deer. A small, paler than normal deer. It looked at me as though it was looking into my soul, before it turned to go back through the trees.'

There was a collective intake of breath around the kitchen table.

'Afterwards – like you two – I just knew everything would be alright. I felt happier and knew I would see you all soon. Five minutes later, you all turned up safe and sound.'

There was complete silence around the table. Even the children knew something important had happened, even if they didn't really understand it. Tears were rolling down Meg's face and were glistening in Fran's eyes.

'Did it have a red nose?' asked Jack.

That broke the spell and everyone laughed at the innocence of children.

'Devin?' said Raff, out of nowhere.

'Sorry?' asked Sadie.

'Devin. It's an old Irish name meaning fawn or small deer. I just wondered if…'

'Perfect!' Fran clapped her hands together while Col clapped him on the back. ''That is just perfect Raff. Thank you.'

Raff smiled his inscrutable smile but Sadie could tell he was really pleased.

'I'm just going to phone Seth now to ask his permission to use his name' said Col and went off into the front room.

'I wonder how long this power cut will last?' said James. 'I've known them last up to twenty-four hours. It's not quite as bad as the 1979 winter out there – but not far off.'

'2010 was a bad one too' added Raff. 'The caravan had eighteen inches of snow on its roof.'

Col came back in, beaming.

'He's really thrilled. I could hear him telling his mum and dad and they sounded really pleased too. They cheered!'

Everyone looked impressed as the solid Yorkshire Dales farming family were not known for displays of emotion, despite being kind and amiable.

'How are they managing with the power cut, I wonder?' asked Sadie.

'They've got a coal-fired range and open fires – they'll be fine. Unlike those with electric ovens' said Em. Then her eyes widened and she looked at Sadie.

'Like Thomas and Joanna…' she added, quietly.

Chapter 17

Thomas answered the phone straight away.

'Hello. Yes. Thomas Poole - Vicar, here.'

'I know it is ' smiled Sadie ' I just phoned you.'

'Ah yes of course. And a HAPPY CHRISTMAS to you ONE AND ALL!' he bellowed down the phone, deafening Sadie.

'Thomas, have you been at the cooking sherry already?' Sadie was laughing now.

'No but that's an excellent idea, don't you think so?' he'd turned his head away, obviously addressing his wife then 'Oh no! – probably not. Definitely not, in fact.'

'Thomas, can you please put Joanna on the phone – and a Happy Christmas to you too.' She wasn't going to get much sense out of him in this mood.

'Yes' he answered, 'It's Phadie on the so…No, erm, Sadie on the phone.'

The next minute, almost before Sadie had recovered from the giggling fit, Joanna's gentle voice, contrasting with that of her husband, could be heard.

'Hello Phadie – and Merry Christmas' she laughed.

'Merry Christmas to you too – and if Thomas has started with his spoonerisms already he's either inebriated or he's absolutely delighted with your special Christmas present' grinned Sadie.

'Oh, he most definitely is.' Joanna said with a chuckle 'and I had a feeling that you knew what it was.'

'I didn't know, I just suspected. But what I'm ringing for is – what are you doing about your Christmas dinner now with the power cut?'

'Ah yes, well, we can't cook the turkey or anything else for that matter. We have a coal fire in the living room but that's about it. I think Thomas has forgotten all about Christmas dinner in the excitement though to be honest.'

'I know you wanted it to be just the two of you this year but, under the circumstances, we would love you to come up here and share our meal with you. There is enough to feed the biblical five thousand, you know what Meg's like. You could bring your turkey here and cook it later, to eat cold tomorrow?'

'Actually, if you don't mind, we would love to do that. It doesn't seem like Christmas without Christmas dinner does it? I'll get Thomas to dig the car out of the driveway…'

'You'll do no such thing' said Sadie in her best bossy-Em voice. 'James is here waiting with his coat on, like a greyhound in the starting traps, ready to fly off when I nod. He's driving Raff's Land Cruiser as it's not blocked in. Em's coming too as she won't let him out of her sight after yesterday.'

'I deny it. I am not a nervous, clingy wife' said Em loudly then looked across at James 'and fasten your coat up and wear your warm hat and be careful you don't slip and …'

James raised his eyes to heaven while Joanna laughed on the other end of the phone.

'Thank you Sadie' she said 'We really appreciate this, especially as all five – no – *six*

– of the Blakemore family are there with you too. How is the baby?'

'You'll see when you come up. James and Em have just gone out of the door so they shouldn't be more than ten minutes, even crawling along. See you soon.'

*

Thomas, entering through the back door, was bouncing like a human pogo stick. Even the children's exuberance had nothing on him.

'We've got some news!' he shouted. Sadie realised that excitement added quite a few decibels to his usual noise level.

'Thomas' chided Joanna 'don't you think we should get in and take our coats off first?'

'Of course, of course' he said, flustered but still with a big silly grin plastered on his face. Sadie chuckled to herself.

'Why don't we all go and sit down in the front room and I'll get everyone a drink?'

'Good idea' said Em, shepherding the three children through – their parents and baby brother following. Joanna pulled Thomas along to see Devin, who was fast asleep in his father's arms. They cooed over him until everyone was seated on the settee, chairs, window seat and floor - and then took their place on the smaller settee.

Sadie held off going for drinks as she didn't think Thomas would be able to wait much longer with his news before exploding.

'Well Thomas, would you like to tell us this news?' she asked.

Thomas looked at Joanna and she nodded at him, linking her arm through his.

'Joanna told me this morning. The best Christmas present ever!' he fidgeted on the settee before finally coming to the point. 'We're going to have a baby!'

The noise that ensued woke Devin but he merely stretched and went straight back to sleep again. Everyone gave their heartfelt congratulations while Sadie and James exchanged a quiet word.

'And there will only be six months between our babies' Thomas beamed, looking over at Col and Devin. 'They'll probably be in the same year at school.'

'You're getting a bit ahead of yourself Thomas' laughed Em, 'you'll be planning his university in an hour and his marriage by the end of the afternoon.'

'It would be nice if they were friends though, wouldn't it?' Fran said as Thomas assured her they would be.

'And if we have a girl, they might become romantically involved?' he gushed.

'Look, I told you – he's planning their marriage already.' said Em.

The next minute, Sadie appeared with a tray of champagne flutes and James followed with two bottles of champagne.

'To wet the baby's head and to celebrate the forthcoming birth of another.'

'This is lovely' said Fran, with Joanna adding her agreement. 'but you shouldn't use your champagne for us.'

'James brought it to celebrate my first Christmas at Acorn Cottage and I can't think of a better way to celebrate it than having the house full of all my favourite people, all safe and happy.'

'I'll drink to that' Raff said, raising his glass to Sadie.

'Cover Devin's ears Col' warned James as the first cork flew over and missed Em's head by a couple of inches.

'Did you do that on purpose, my sweet?' said Em, casting her beady eye towards James.

'I did, my beloved' he replied 'although I expected you to catch it in your teeth.'

'He's lived with you too long' Meg said as she shook her head sadly at Em.

Chapter 18

'Another two hours and then I want you all sitting down at the table, hands washed and appetites sharp. Do you hear that everyone?'

Meg shouted down the hallway so that whoever was left in the sitting room – mostly now discussing babies – heard her too.

'She's getting quite militant isn't she? I'm sure she had a previous life as one of my dinner ladies' laughed Sadie.

'Anything to do with food and she turns into Attila the Hun.' Em replied.

Raff turned from washing up redundant pans – his servant duties.

'Time to take the dogs up the garden?' he asked Sadie.

'Of course' she replied.

It would be nice to get Raff to herself for a while. She pulled her coat and boots on. 'Up' the garden meant towards the gypsy caravan, a longer distance than 'down' the garden, which meant the front of the cottage.

'Where's my hat?' she asked, checking her pockets again.

'Ah' Raff replied with a guilty look on his face, 'the snowman's need was greater than yours.'

'The snowman is wearing my hat?'

'He's wearing my scarf though' Raff tried to make things sound better ' and he's smoking Em's pipe.'

'I thought you'd stopped that filthy habit?' James addressed his wife.

'No, you were the filthy habit I tried to stop but I married you instead' she threw back at him.

'Raff means the twig that Em found that looks like a pipe.' Meg explained to Sadie then shook her head. The children were far better behaved than this lot.

Now Whisky and Bran had seen what fun the snow could be, it wasn't hard to drag them outside and they came running willingly as Raff held the door open and called their names. They ran onto the large terrace, down the steps and proceeded to find every untrodden patch of virgin snow to run round in circles on or bounce into.

Raff and Sadie wandered up the garden, holding hands. She still felt a thrill just in this one simple act. She knew it wasn't a natural thing to do for Raff. As kind, thoughtful and loving as he was, he was also an enigma in that he didn't like showing his feelings. He didn't seem to have been hurt in the past, or at least if he had, he hadn't talked about it. His parents and grandparents both had particularly romantic stories – but he was very reluctant to show his emotions.

He had a huge streak of independence which possibly came from his gypsy heritage as well as the Celtic cussedness. He could also have occasional bouts of moodiness which gave him a dark edge but he never took it out on Sadie, or anyone else. The moods were turned inwards and he was never anything less than a gentlemen in his dealings with people – unless he thought they deserved it.

Sadie understood the emotional reluctance. After her last experience of relationships when her fiancé, despite being a balder version of Mr.

Bean (what was she thinking!) had an affair, she had decided that being on her own was the best thing.

Raff had changed her mind as she had changed his – but they were still both their own people. Weren't they? She held his hand tighter and he turned to her and smiled. God, she thought, he was so good-looking!

They walked past the 'Dovecote' nearby. This was Em's glass-roofed studio that Sadie had renovated and presented to her – much to Em's delight. Not least because it meant they saw each other at least four of the working days. Unless Em was deep into a commissioned piece and then all her concentration was on that – and woe betide anyone who interrupted her. James and Sadie had developed an 'Em radar' which kept them well out of the way on those particular days. The remaining day Em used to take commissions out or liaise with customers. The weekend belonged to her and James.

'Are you going to check the cabin again?' asked Sadie, frowning as he nodded.

He usually checked it every day if he was staying with Sadie and most of his clothes were still in his wardrobe there. Sadie did the same when she stayed at the cabin. They joked that not many couples had the choice of two homes but they could tell that most people thought it was a strange arrangement. Perhaps the truth was that they were both scared. Scared of commitment, scared of putting all their eggs in one basket. Scared even of trusting anyone – putting their happiness in the hands of another.

Sadie took another sidelong glance at him as he walked, still firmly holding on to her hand. She knew they loved each other and that should be enough without thinking what separate dwellings meant. They were hardly ever apart, after all. They reached the clearing to the left, where the caravan was.

'Do you think there's eighteen inches of snow on it this year too?' he asked, scrutinising the bowed roof and the snow piled up on it.

'Just about, I think' said Sadie as she gingerly climbed the slippy steps and holding on to the double door handles as she reached them, she peered in. 'Did you bring your key?'

'Yes but we won't let any cold air in just now. Does everything look okay?' He joined her at the windows.

'It looks fine. Still cosy. I think you'd need an extra blanket on the bed though, if you wanted a night communing with nature at the moment'

She smiled to herself and looked further down at the wooden bed built into the far end, with its window looking out to the west to catch the sunsets. This window they were gazing through, caught the sunrises. As much as she adored Acorn Cottage, this place and the nights they spent here together, mostly in the summer months, would always hold a place in her heart.

Her eyes went to the seats at the side. Patchwork cushions and patchwork seat pads that Raff's mother had made. On the bookshelves hung lace edging from his great-grandmother and on the dresser were embroidered cloths, made by his grandmother.

Even in the dark interior, Sadie could see the polished wood shining and could almost smell the lavender beeswax that Raff lovingly kept up with, as well as black-leading the iron stove, its chimney climbing up the side and out of the roof. This caravan was part of his Gypsy heritage and its upkeep was important to him.

As they climbed down and set off by the edge of the field for the cabin, Sadie could see the old barn, set behind it in which Raff did his wood crafts and commissions. It was almost as big as the cabin itself and included a double garage at the far end.

A few minutes later they unlocked the cabin door. Inside, the interior looked more like a Swiss chalet than the Swedish cabin he had built it as. It had upside down living and, as they climbed the stairs to the kitchen with its balcony looking out over Mab's Wood and beyond, Sadie saw there were boxes of vegetables along the work surfaces – and a sack of potatoes standing against a floor cupboard. It looked like he'd brought everything in from the storage shed, thought Sadie, puzzled. They had more than enough already at the cottage.

As her eyes roamed around the large room, they stopped dead at the sight outside the bedroom they used. Raff's bedroom. There was a very large suitcase on wheels there, that looked to be filled to bursting point. Beside it was a large backpack of the type you'd use on a gap year in Bali.

Sadie felt a sudden jolt of fear. Was this why Raff hadn't been himself today and had taken so long up here this morning? Was he going away? If so, why hadn't he told her before it had come to this stage? Her eyes moved slowly from the suitcase towards Raff, who she realised was standing quite still and looking straight at her. Their eyes met and Sadie held her breath.

Raff tore his eyes away from her and indicated the table in front of the window.

'Sit down Sadie. I want to talk to you. I have something planned. Perhaps not planned exactly as it's a bit spur of the moment – but I'm not sure how you're going to take it. It will affect us both.'

He held his hand out towards the table and robotically and incapable of speech, Sadie made her way there, not meeting his eyes.

Chapter 19

Whisky looked at Bran with doleful eyes. Their master and mistress – as they liked to think of themselves – were taking a long time inside the cabin.

This playing in the snow lark was alright if you had something to do, thought Whisky, *but not if you were just trotting around investigating strange-smelling yellow holes in the snow for the umpteenth time while you were waiting – and they still smelt of him and Bran anyway.*

Occasionally they caught a whiff of a strange animal and it sent them into waves of delight that only turning round at least three times on the spot could alleviate.

Now though, a little independent thought was required. Whisky looked at Bran and wiggled his ears. Bran frowned. *Oh honestly,* thought Whisky, *I thought these sheepdogs were supposed to be intelligent.*

Although Bran was probably only being cautious as he was a steadying influence on him. Or so the humans thought. Whisky rather thought that he had an un-steadying influence on Bran.

This time he cocked his head to one side and raised one eyebrow. Bran gave him a big grin in return, the way only sheepdogs can.

At last, the sheepdog gets it!, thought Whisky, running in the direction of the front garden and the snowman. Bran followed on.

I'll humour the boy, he thought**, let him think he's got his own way – but I'll have to think of a way to deflect his attention from the task he has planned, or there will be no Christmas treat for either of us.**

Whisky ran full pelt down to the cottage, executed a doggie-triple salko as he negotiated the corner at the wrong angle and finally, came in sight of his goal…the snowman.

Whisky stood, four paws planted deep in the snow and head down, making a last minute decision. Should he go for the snowman's bottom and let it collapse that way or should he make a leap for the head and demolish it from the top down? The second option was more exciting so he steeled himself, setting his small shoulders and leaning his body back so he could get the height, to reach…

Woof! Woof, woof woof!

What was that? What was the sheepdog doing? Was he mad? They had to keep quiet or they wouldn't get away with it if they were caught in the act. If they weren't they could blame it on some very aggressive rabbits that had wandered into the garden.

There, that should alert them, thought Bran, ***Sorry my friend but you'll thank me when you're eating your ultra-large, turkey-flavoured chew bone later on.***

Whisky turned back after glaring at his friend with a malevolent look he'd been practising in front of the hall mirror. He turned once more to face his snowman prey and steeled himself.

And here he comes, up for the high jump title, the reigning champion – it's Whisky Norwood himself!

Rocking backwards and forwards on his back paws, he chose his moment then flung himself forward. His front paws left the ground.

Is it a bird? Is it a plane? No – it's …

'Whisky! Don't you dare!' came the authoritarian tones of Em, delivered at one hundred and twenty decibels from the front door.

Whisky faltered mid-flight, missed his objective by a few inches and landed in an undignified heap, his nose in the snow and his tail sticking out like a beacon.

'Well done Bran' laughed James, knowingly as he joined his wife on the front terrace.

'You little Tyke!' shouted Em to the soggy sight that emerged from the snow, then she bent down and threw a snowball at him. Gathering his punctured pride, Whisky made a half-hearted jump to catch the snowball in his mouth before it disintegrated around him.

Oh, he thought, *this is fun, in a sadistic kind of way* - and he stood waiting for another, ears pricked in expectation. Em obliged. Bran ran down to join in the fun and James threw one at him, the snow cascading on his black shoulders as he 'caught' it.

A few minutes later, curiosity brought the three older Blakemore children to the door and soon, the front garden was a scene of chaos – screams, laughter and barks – as snowballs were thrown at the dogs and each other.

Sadie and Raff appeared, hand in hand, from the side of the house and stood with Meg at the front door, surveying the scene.

'We could hear the noise from over near the caravan' said Raff, 'so we came to investigate. We thought the circus had arrived.'

'I think it has' said Meg in resignation, watching the snowballs fly across the garden. 'The children started it.'

There was a meaningful pause then Sadie turned towards Meg.

'You mean Em and James don't you?'

'Of course. That's taken for granted.'

Sadie grinned and debated joining in but time was getting on and she had to go inside and help Meg now.

'It will be dinner in an hour. Do you think they will all be dried off by then?' sighed Meg.

Sadie smiled and gave her a hug, steering her back inside,

'Don't worry, all will be well.'

Chapter 20

Everyone entered the dining room in reverent silence apart from a few intakes of breath. The scene that met them was magnificent. The fire burned brightly in the dog-grate and the whole room seemed to glow in a golden warmth.

A long, white damask tablecloth covered the long oak table and a red and gold brocade runner was displayed along the centre. On that were placed two large candles in tall candlesticks that threw light on the table. These added to the tealights in the berry jars on the runner. The crystal glasses reflected the flickering lights, heightening their effect.

Above the table, the berry lights were giving off a soft red light as they hung down from the two redundant overhead lights. Pure white charger plates stood, shining in readiness on red damask place mats while Christmas crackers in red and green waited to supply the usual terrible jokes.

At the windows, Sadie's hastily improvised fairy lights magnified the gathering darkness, whilst the snow itself reflected the lights shining down on it from within. The Christmas tree dominated the far corner and a string of emergency fairy lights was twisted artfully around it, highlighting the red baubles and shimmering on their shiny surfaces. The children's iced cookie baubles took pride of place at the front of the tree.

Everyone sat down now in the places designated by their snowman place markers, the children exclaiming with glee as they found their own names. Small dishes of avocado and prawn salad appeared before them like magic. Crackers were held up to neighbours and silly hats were worn.

Raff predictably read the first awful joke out, (What do you call a snowman in a heatwave?...Water!). James opened a bottle of good sparkling wine, the popping sound of which Devin took in his stride with hardly a blink, while Em filled the children's glasses with sparkling strawberry-flavoured water.

Finally, Meg and Sadie took their places at the table and held their glasses up for the toast. And then the lights came back on.

*

Later, after the main meal had been served, Sadie sat back in her chair allowing her stomach room to expand. They were all taking a little time before they could manage pudding as they wanted to do full justice to Meg's delicious food.

Sadie tuned out of the conversation, smiling instead at the memory of the laughter that greeted her reaction to the end of the power cut.

'I'm not having that!' she had said in a fit of pique and had immediately turned off every lamp and light on in the place that had dared to come back on, apart from the electrical fairy lights. You can never have too many fairy lights, she thought again, as they would be double strength now round the trees and elsewhere. They all agreed with her though that it looked far more intimate and cosy in candlelight.

The meal had looked – and tasted – magnificent, The huge lemon and thyme-basted turkey took up most of the middle of the table with the maple-glazed ham and the slow-roasted pork with separate crispy crackling at either end. At a decent distance away from the meat was the Blakemore's nut roast, which actually looked really delicious and even James declared it so when he pinched a bit off Lucy's plate.

There were tureens full of crispy roast potatoes with thyme, then roasted parsnips and Chantilly carrots in a honey glaze. There was one of sprouts with chestnuts and one with spiced red cabbage. Not forgetting the Yorkshire puddings for a proper Yorkshire Christmas! Around the turkey were bacon-wrapped chipolatas and there were two large jugs of Meg's special gravy. On the side table were bowls of cranberry sauce, apple sauce, bread sauce and a jar of mustard.

Nobody could move now. Em said she had wanted to go to the loo twenty minutes ago but it might be midnight before she could get off the chair.

Sadie smiled to herself. This Christmas Day had gone even better than she could ever have hoped for. Despite all the fates conspiring against it in the form of demon blizzards, dangerous rescue missions, unexpected births and power cuts – she couldn't have planned a better day than the one she'd had. She sighed happily and looking round, caught Raff's eye as he grinned at her. He knew what she was thinking. They were almost telepathic sometimes. Then she noticed his expression turn to one of alarm and, leaning forward, she tuned back in to the conversation.

'…up a tree covered in snow, in blizzard conditions…' she heard.

Sadie frowned, puzzled. Understanding gradually settled on her as she took in Raff's panicked expression at her side as he checked her out.

'Sorry' she said calmly, 'I missed the first bit Col, can you repeat it? '

Col was about to do as instructed when he caught sight of Raff's face and faltered.

'Erm …' he managed.

James jumped in to save the poor man further embarrassment.

166

'It was after we found the van and knew that everyone was okay. Raff was desperate to let you know all was well so far, as he knew you and Em would be worried.'

'Yes' said Sadie, 'we were. And…?

James knew that tone. She was more like Em than she knew.

'We'd learnt from Col that he had tried everywhere to get a signal but – Raff thought he might be able to get one higher up.'

'Uh-huh' said Sadie, listening to James but watching Raff as he looked as uncomfortable as she'd ever seen him.

'Well, he saw a tree that looked easy enough to climb to try for a signal. So he did.'

Sadie nodded.

'So he climbed, nearly to the top as it happened and managed to get a signal. We could hear him faintly, talking to someone. So it was all fine' smiled James and then, being the most honest of men, unfortunately went on. 'Mind you, when he slipped on the way down and ended up hanging by one hand, we were a little alarmed but he managed to swing himself onto another branch so it turned out well.'

James smiled benevolently around his companions..

There was a hush as everyone looked at Sadie, feeling her silence. She shook her head then looked up, green eyes blazing. Without a word, she turned to Raff in the next seat and leant forward until she was a few inches away from the whites of his eyes. Then she flung her arms around him and kissed him fervently and from the heart.

Lucy and Izzy looked at each other and put their fingers down their throat to mimic being sick and Jack just said 'Yuk!'.

'I love you for worrying so much about us that you would even do a stupid thing like that' whispered Sadie 'but if you ever, EVER...'

'I cannot see that situation ever arising again, so I can almost one hundred percent promise you that I won't.'

Raff pulled her into him for another kiss and Em now joined the children in sticking her fingers down her throat too while everyone else cheered. Thomas even pulled Joanna in for a kiss too, which made her blush even though she looked pleased. As Sadie sat back in her seat, she looked across at Em, who smiled and raised her glass. She understood.

'Another drink anyone?' asked James, relief flooding his face.

'Yes please' chorused Sadie and Em.

They had been reliving last night in their heads for the last minute or two and wanted to blot it out.

Raff wasn't drinking as he was on driving duty. This made Sadie think.

'Does the power coming on mean your heating will come on now Thomas?' she asked.

'No but I can just reset it' he replied 'and it will heat up quickly. Yours too Col?'

'I'm afraid ours is a little more complicated' he said, not pursuing his statement.

There was silence until a little voice interrupted.

'When can we have pudding?' came Jack's plaintive cry.

Chapter 21

Ten minutes later they were all sitting with a traditional Christmas pud in front of them and a jug of hot, creamy custard. In front of the children sat a fruit trifle, full of raspberries in jelly and decorated with sprinkles and cherries. Sadie and Meg debated on bringing the chocolate roulade through with Irish cream sauce in a jug but decided that would be better for supper as everyone would be over-faced with it.

Meg, like all good cooks liked to feed people so they were full to the brim and consequently made more than anyone could eat. Most of it could be frozen though. She had become an expert since Em bought her a Freezer book for reference as Em hated waste.

Afterwards, Devin had his Christmas dinner as Fran had sat in the comfy chair next to the windows and fed him whilst looking out into the snowy surrounds. At least no more snow had appeared, although this lot didn't seem to be disappearing at all. It was hard to tell as gardens could look completely snowbound even when main roads had been cleared by snow ploughs or by the level of traffic on them. It was Christmas though and there wouldn't be many cars on the road even under normal circumstances.

Joanna looked at Raff's glass of water. He had drunk one glass to toast Sadie's first Christmas here but after that, had stuck to water. It made her feel guilty.

'We're curtailing your Christmas drinks Raff. We will go home whenever you are ready and then you can celebrate properly' she said.

Colin looked at Fran solemnly, then spoke,

'Us too Raff. We are eternally grateful for everything you have done for us this Christmas but we really don't want to impose on you all any more than we already have.'

'You haven't imposed on us at all, have they Sadie?' said Em and Sadie agreed vehemently.

'You are all so kind but we have intruded on your Christmas too long' said Fran.

Sadie put her hands up to silence everyone. It worked.

'Can I just let you all know - and I know that I speak for Raff, James …and Seth too, that far from ruining anyone's Christmas, you have all *made* it. Having you all here has just been like one big, family celebration. As Em will testify, family – and celebrations -were things that were sorely missing in my life until I came here. You've provided the big gathering I hoped for and given me the best Christmas I can ever remember.

'Well said' smiled Em and everyone raised their glasses.

'You're all so kind, how will we ever repay you' said Fran, tears glistening in her eyes.

'You really are' said Thomas, smiling benevolently at Sadie.

'Enough' said Em, doing a scissors motion with her arms. 'We'll all be crying into our wine soon. I think I speak for Sadie and all when I say that these things are not done because repayment is expected but because of even more selfish reasons. Having you all here adds to our enjoyment. It isn't in any way a burden. What James, Raff and Seth did yesterday was because they wanted to and not because they had to. More importantly, they did it because they knew that you would do the same for them without a second thought. So pipe down the lot of you and help me drink this excellent brandy before I break the habit of a lifetime and get emotional.'

'And bossy' said James.

'That's a given' she said and leaned into his shoulder as he went to give her a hug, kissing the top of her head.

Raff brought the emotion to an end before the children stopped looking merely puzzled and started asking questions about exactly why their parents were so grateful. That was a conversation for another day, when they were all settled.

'I am ready to take you all home whenever you are ready but I hope you're not running off straight after dinner. Come and relax with us for a while.'

'At least now the power is back on Col, you will soon be back to normal at home' beamed Thomas.

Raff looked at Col, who looked at Fran. None of them seemed to be happy. Thomas's smile wavered.

'Well actually, because we have storage heaters, the power cut will have thrown the timings all out of kilter. We will have to reset them when we get back in and we probably won't be warm for a while' confessed Col, then seeing everyone's worried expression, added 'but it will be fine, we have lots of extra blankets at home.'

Raff's eyes met Sadie's and she smiled and nodded. He cleared his throat, nervous as he knew how independent Col and Fran were and especially in the light of their 'repayment' talk. He took a deep breath.

'I have a proposition for you. It is entirely up to you whether or not you want to act on it as I know you have your pride. I admire that. We all do – but let me tell you what it is.'

The entire room was silent and every face was turned towards Raff.

'When I went into your cottage with you Col, for the first time I saw the conditions your landlady has you live in. There was damp on the walls, the place was freezing and the rooms are tiny, too small to accommodate you before and now, with the baby…

I had been deliberating on my situation for a while and even though *your* situation didn't force me into it in any way' he looked at Sadie to make sure she understood this, 'it did spur me on to make my mind up at last.

Therefore, if you decide it's right for you, I'd like to offer you the tenancy of my cabin, at the top of Mab's Wood.'

Fran and Col turned and stared at each other, eyes wide, grabbing each other's hands tightly before turning back to Raff.

'But we couldn't…'

'Yes you could. Why not? I hardly use it now as I spend more of my time here at Acorn Cottage. The cabin needs to be lived in or it will get that sad, decaying feel about it. It needs to be lived in- and loved. You would be helping me too. You only need pay the same rent as you do with the cottage you're in now but, as with there, you will have to pay all the utility bills etc. Which, I have to say will be far more economical than that cottage as I built it as an eco-house.'

Fran and Col's mouths were open, only a fraction more than everyone else's.

'You can also have the use of my van, which has a double row of seats to fit the family in – but there is a catch. When I need a commission delivering, I would expect you to do it. Petrol paid. Only three or four times a month usually but it could be anywhere in the country. It takes me away from my work and I could do with the help.'

There was a pause when no-one said a word.

'Is that alright?' asked Raff uncertainly. 'No pressure at all'

Col held his wife's hand so tightly there was a danger of cutting her circulation off.

'Alright?' he breathed 'Are you joking? There is no place for pride in the situation we are in. Raff, my friend, you are the answer to our prayers. This is twice you've come to our rescue in two days.'

Everyone let out the collective breath they had been holding. This wonderful, free-spirited, old-hippie-type couple were notoriously self-reliant. Which is why Raff was pussy-footing around with his offer. For them to accept showed just how bad the situation must have been for them.

As an emotional Col leant forward to grasp Raff's hand in a firm handshake, a little voice piped up,

'Does that mean we can have Bran and Whisky too?'

Raff grinned.

'I'm sure you can share them Jack' he said. 'I'm sure they'd love to play in Mab's Wood with you all.

Chapter 22

The lantern-lit journey up to the cabin was short and very sweet.

The Blakemore's were all singing 'Ding Dong Merrily on High'. Sadie could almost see the metaphorical weight lifting from their shoulders with this unexpected answer to their problems.

The children had all come out with their backpacks on and carrying their iced baubles from the tree. Raff was carrying Jack on his shoulders. This was the right decision, in more ways than one. Little Devin's face peeped out of the blanket as he was carried in his carry cot. He had certainly had an interesting debut into this world.

None of the family had been in Raff's cabin before although Col had often been in his woodworking barn, collecting offcuts from

Raff's larger projects to use for his own crafts. They both had a fascination for the feel of wood and how it could be used. They had spent a lot of time discussing it inside the barn over mugs of tea. Their first sight of the cabin though was now – and they stopped, reduced to silence. Wow was the only word that could be heard.

Raff made vague gestures to the right, left and ahead like a particularly macho airline steward.

'Bedroom there, bedroom there, small study or extra single bedroom there, bathroom and utility room at the end, then here…'

They followed him up the bespoke wooden stairs, open-mouthed at what they saw at the top. Warmth emanated both from the underfloor heating and the look of the light wooden surrounds.

'Here' he continued, 'is the open plan kitchen, dining room and living room. Double bedroom ensuite there' he pointed to his bedroom.

Indicating the boxes of fresh produce scattered around the work surface he said,

'Help yourself to those and any other food you see in the cupboards and fridge. We have more than enough at Acorn Cottage.'

'Here's the veggie lasagne that Meg gave you, if you put it in the fridge now, it will be defrosted for tomorrow, along with the other bag of stuff she gave us to bring up' Sadie grinned, 'Meg's not happy unless she's feeding people.'

Fran looked to be close to tears again. Col gave her a hug.

'It's beyond our wildest dreams Raff. Just *slightly* better than our other place...' he said with ironic understatement.

'Can we choose our bedrooms Dad?' Lucy, Izzy and Jack set up a chorus – a wall of noise.

'Apart from the one here with the ensuite which will be ours, away from you noisy lot' laughed Col.

'Me and Izzy will share the biggest one' said Lucy, decisively.

'But Dev will be sharing with me too' Jack answered back, 'so we will need a big one too.'

'They're both the same size. Two twin rooms big enough to fit you all in' smiled Raff.

'And I think Devin will be sleeping with us for a little while Jack but he can come in with you as soon as he's ready.' Fran told Jack, who seemed happy with the explanation.

'Won't you need your clothes from your bedroom Raff?' she added.

'Sadie and I dragged it all down today before dinner, after which we realised that wheels were no good in deep snow and we should have used a sledge strapped on to Bran and Whisky like a couple of oddly matched huskies. Right, we'll be going now. Anything you need to know, we're at the other end of the phone.

The weather gurus say the thaw has started but I'm not sure if they've factored in the micro-climate of the Yorkshire Dales, although the twenty-seventh is supposed to be much better. Jez rang and the snow ploughs and gritters are coming out over these two neighbouring dales too – unsung heroes all. So you should be able to get the van from the barn and fetch the rest of your stuff from the old place. The van keys are with the house keys, clearly marked. Any problems, let me know.'

Col grabbed Raff in a surprise bear hug. Sadie thought the gesture was hiding his face which had started crumpling up with emotion just before. Fran had noticed too and diffused the situation.

'Don't forget to say thank you to Sadie for your Christmas presents' she said to the children.

'We *did*!' said Jack very truthfully'

The girls thanked her again and waved their arms to show the daisy and the yellow rose bracelets she had given them. They had been very proud of the first acquisition for their jewellery boxes. Jack too, had got very excited by the brightly coloured 'jewels' for his pirate's chest.

'Thank you again for the buried pirate's treasure' Jack said, 'especially as I've nearly eaten all the chocolate coins now.'

Sadie laughed, then Fran whispered 'And thank you for the silver deer charm for Devin. It will remind him throughout his life of the circumstances of his birth and the kind people who surrounded him on his very first Christmas.'

'And thank Auntie Joanna again' said the girls, reaching into a bag and grabbing two identical knitted dolls apart from one had a pink dress and one had a lilac dress.

'Yes, me too' Jack shouted, holding up a knitted Spiderman and giving it a hug.

Sadie and Raff went down to the front door with the children clattering behind them on their way to stake claims on the bedrooms.

'Oh' said Raff, backing up to Col, 'the kids can play in Mab's Wood this end up to the fence, as I own it. The entrance and exit to the cabin is down the driveway on the right which leads to the lane, so you don't have to come the way we arrived today.'

Then they went out into the snow yet again.

'I think I may have to put a gate across here' he said, indicating the opening to the caravan's clearing from the small field that led to his cabin, 'to separate the clearing and Acorn Cottage off from the rest, so they know the boundaries.'

'Are you worried about the caravan? The children don't seem the destructive type, I'm sure it will be safe' said Sadie.

'It's not that, it's if we want to use it from Spring onwards to watch the sun at solstice, have a campfire supper or…for anything else we can think of – then we don't have to worry about anyone popping up round the corner. Much as I love that family, my privacy is still important to me, in the context of the caravan at least.'

'Especially when it's being used … 'for anything else we can think of…' she grinned.

'Exactly' winked Raff, 'That particular pastime was uppermost in my mind. I'm sure Col would agree with me in relation to that. To make sure it doesn't sound unfriendly instead of merely practical, I can make part of the fence to Mab's Court car park into a gate so they can walk down through Mab's Wood, across the little field- and they will be at work. They won't even have to use the van. Even the school is within easy walking distance, no further than from their old cottage.'

'Perfect Raff'

'I know I am' he said, flicking his hair back in a surf dude imitation and flexing his muscles.

'Did I say I loved your modesty too' she asked.

'My modesty is just one of the wonderful and admirable things about me, along with my dazzling good looks.'

'Mm, can't deny the last observation' she sighed, pulling him down towards her for a lingering kiss.

'There's no rush is there? To get back home?' he sneaked a look back at the caravan.

'You'd have to have that woodburner lit before you could have your wicked way with me in there today' Sadie replied.

'So unromantic. Where's your sense of adventure?' Raff pretended to be hurt.

'I'm sure it will come back when I'm warm' she said.

They leaned in for another kiss, then strode down, arm in arm, towards the cottage.

Chapter 23

When Sadie and Raff entered the kitchen, they found Meg still cleaning down the surfaces and the dishwasher humming away to itself.

'Meg! Leave that now, have a rest for heaven's sake.' Sadie took the cloth from her and guided her, protesting, towards the sitting room where she could hear Em and James talking.

As they entered, Em turned to Sadie.

'We can turn off all the lamps now you're here if you like, so you don't have another meltdown?'

Sadie laughed.

'It was not a melt-down, it was merely bad timing on the electric's part. We've still got candles burning anyway and double fairy lights on the tree. We'll perhaps need more light if we're going to play board games? Did Thomas and Joanna get home alright?'

'Yes' replied Em 'we dropped them off and the roads are no worse. Thomas hasn't come down from the ceiling yet. I'm convinced he'll still be bouncing about at 2 a.m. He's so excited about the baby news.'

'I know' Sadie smiled 'and so is Joanna in a much more reserved way. That was what was wrong with her when she was 'ill' in the mornings.'

'Did you know?' asked James.

'No, I just guessed. It was the Christmas present bit that made me think. Joanna was determined that there should be just the two of them when she gave him his present. So unless Joanna had bought a Christmas bunny-girl costume for Thomas's delectation, then it had to be something good that she wanted to tell him privately.'

'I'm so pleased for them' said Meg.

'As are we all' agreed Em ' and Sadie, are you sure you still want us here after the two days you've had?'

Em, James and Meg were staying until after Boxing Day breakfast. That was planned even before the snows came.

'Of course we do, we're looking forward to the silly games night.' Then a thought hit her. 'Unless you've had enough and want to go home for a bit of peace and quiet? It's been a busy couple of days for all of *you* as well.'

'No, I'm looking forward to beating you all' said Em and the others agreed they wanted to stay.

'I think Em was just worried you might want privacy to show your *own* bunny-girl costume to Raff' said James. Living with Em was definitely rubbing off on him.

'I was more worried about all the rubber fetish gear we found in the study' countered Em.

'I *told* you to hide it in the bedroom' added Raff, winking at Sadie.

'Oh you're all as bad' sighed Meg, despairing.

Em stood up and whispered to Sadie,

'Talking of the study…'

'Ah yes' she said and led Em into the room across the hallway.

Sadie switched on the light as they entered. This was the only room downstairs that hadn't been decorated for Christmas. Now, Sadie bent to retrieve a large basket of Christmas flowers – winter roses, gerbera, chrysanthemums, carnations and berries along with Christmas foliage and pine cones for decoration – with a card placed at the top.

Em was looking at the A4 notebooks on top of the desk, next to a huge, ancient, leather tome and some research books.

'You're still writing your book then?' she asked Sadie.

'Trying to, yes. I'm not sure whether to make it just a family history or make it an herbal text book as well. Both aspects are so fascinating.'

The leather 'spell book' was written in the sixteenth century by Sarah Norwood, who was writing down the 'spells' of her grandmother Agnes from an earlier time. It was probably dictated by Agnes when she was very old and was worried about the information being lost. She will have wanted it to continue through the generations to come.

Agnes was a direct ancestor of both Sadie and Em and she was possibly the first owner of Acorn Cottage. Apart from standing empty in recent years - a blip in its timeline- it had stayed in the Norwood family ever since.

The book was full of healing potions and remedies, as well as which herbs to grow, all of which could easily have got Agnes taken away as a 'witch' if discovered. The Norwoods had a reputation as healers – and as witches by extension – because of their skill with herbs. Sadie was carrying the tradition on by growing herbs around the Brighid statue, Agnes's original herb garden, and selling them in her shop in various forms. On account of the juxtaposition of Brighid's statue and Agnes's herb garden, the two female figures were forever associated in Sadie's mind.

'Why don't you write two books?' Em said 'One for the family history and another for the herbs? Seems sensible to me.'

Sadie sighed.

'Yes, it does seem sensible – just twice the work.' She brightened up 'Worth it though, maybe?'

Em nodded as she grabbed hold of one side of the basket and they went back into the room.

'Meg?' Meg turned around at the sound of Sadie's voice. 'We'd like to give you this to thank you for all you've done today and yesterday. I'm not exaggerating when I say we really couldn't have managed without you. Not just for all the cooking, baking and serving out you've been doing but because you are an integral part of our family. Thank you so much, from all of us.'

By this time, the tears were rolling down Meg's cheeks. Next to food, she loved flowers and had already transformed her small garden in Em's old cottage.

'Oh' Meg sniffed. 'That's beautiful – and there's a card.'

'Open it' said James.

Meg opened it to find a voucher for an upmarket kitchenware store in Gressleigh.

'Oh, just brilliant!' breathed Meg.

'But don't use it to get any of these' Em said, handing over a wrapped box.

Meg tore the paper off like she was five years old.

'It's those kitchen knives I was wanting! I can't believe you remembered' said Meg, taking the smallest one out of the block and examining it lovingly.

'I'm not so sure she should have extra sharp kitchen knives around her when she's in one of her 'food-aggressive' moods' frowned Em.

'I do *not* get aggressive' Meg brandished the knife uncomfortable close to Em's nose.

'You've made your point' punned Em as everyone groaned.

'Raff and I also bought you that big, glazed ceramic planter you wanted for the garden, Meg. We would have handed it over to you today but as we couldn't get through to the garden centre because of the snow, they've said they'll deliver it to Church View Cottage as soon as the roads are clear enough.'

'That's *wonderful*!' gushed Meg. 'I wanted it to plant my Yakushima in.'

'As you do…' said Em.

There followed the present-giving they hadn't found the time for earlier.

Em and James were delighted with the stained glass window that Sadie and Raff had commissioned from Em's friend Artie, who had one of the courtyard units. It had their names and the date of their marriage – and was destined for the new summerhouse they were building at Winterhill Lodge in the Spring.

'I've had Artie and Bill conferring on window sizes so it will fit one of the side windows easily' explained Raff. Bill was one of the joiners who worked part-time at Winterhill Manor and used to work for James, so was now going to build the summerhouse for them.

Sadie and Raff received a luxury edition of Scrabble with a wood and brass base. They loved it and laughed as they had become quite competitive over their Scrabble games.

Meg had given the same present to each couple. A 1950s-style Roberts radio, which also went down very well. Em had already earmarked hers for her Dovecote studio but compromised on bringing it back in the evenings and on weekends for James too.

'How about using our new Scrabble board instead of Trivial Pursuit?' asked Sadie.

'You can only have up to four players remember' said Raff.

Meg looked sheepish then spoke up.

'Would you all mind if I didn't play? I'm not very good at these games and I'm always glad when I invariably lose first so I can sit out and do something else.' Meg was the least competitive person ever if it didn't involve food.

'But we don't want to leave you out' said Sadie 'Is there anything else you want to play?'

'Actually' Meg went on, looking embarrassed 'The Bishop's Wife with David Niven and Loretta Young – and Cary Grant – is on TV soon and I absolutely love that film so I was hoping…'

'Of course Meg, if you're happy doing that? I'll get the right channel for you.'

Raff pointed to the comfortable chair next to the flickering wood burner and she settled down into it willingly.

'I think we'd better play this in the kitchen, remembering how loud and unruly we get during a game' James suggested.

'Would you mind if we left you in peace to watch it?' asked Sadie.

'Hmm?' said Meg, distractedly, 'Oh, not at all'

So they all trooped through with both dogs following them out, with a look on their faces that said 'What about us?'

'We forgot the dogs!' said Raff, who was obviously adept at reading dog-expressions.

James set the Scrabble board up while the others gave out the doggie Christmas presents. New collars for them both, a cuddly toy each that they could shake furiously from side to side to their heart's content – and two large turkey-flavoured chew bones.

'Drinks before we start in earnest?' asked Sadie and while Raff filled their glasses, Sadie went through to ask Meg if she wanted one too.

She found her, head back against the comfortable cushions, eyes closed, mouth open and gently snoring – with the opening titles of The Bishop's Wife rolling up the screen. Sadie smiled and backed out. She would buy her the DVD if she wanted it, or if not, it was bound to be repeated but for now, if anyone needed her sleep, it was Meg.

On their beds in front of the Aga, warm and happy and gnawing their chew bones, lay the two furry ones. Bran looked at the small Cairn terrier across from him.

You see, young fella-me-dog, if you had demolished the snowman, you would have been eating a small dog biscuit if you were lucky, instead of this.

Whisky raised hairy doggy brows at the sheepdog.

I bow-wow to your superior knowledge on this one occasion, my friend. Merry Christmas!

Chapter 24

Boxing Day

Everyone sat around the table, either yawning or lethargic after a late night – except Meg. She had slept the sleep of the righteous. She was bright-eyed and bushy-tailed after sleeping solidly through The Bishop's Wife, It's a Wonderful Life, Elf and all the Christmas versions of soaps and reality programmes.

She had also slept through the deluge of protests and laughter at Em's Scrabble words and the raucous karaoke that followed on. She also slept through the barking of Whisky and Bran who didn't want to be left out of the Christmas night fun and had a mad half hour chasing each other round the kitchen during the karaoke, just to prove that 'dogs just wanna have fu-un' too.

She only half-woke up as Em and James dragged her bodily up the stairs to her bedroom -and she only woke up, as fresh as a daisy, at seven a.m. Then she proceeded to wake everyone else up as she clattered pots and pans around. However much they tried to ignore it, the inviting smell drifted up to them and in the next twenty minutes, they all drifted gradually downstairs.

There was also a big coffee pot full of enticingly strong ground coffee. Just what they all needed.

Even though they had all been eating turkey sandwiches long after midnight last night, the large tin of freshly made ham and mushroom frittata that Meg placed in front of them, set their appetites off again.

Meg fluttered round them like a plump and happy house-fairy. She had finished 'Hark the Herald Angels Sing' and then had started singing 'All Christian Men Rejoice' and had now started singing 'In Dulci Jubilo', which came out as a mixture of words and some 'hum-hums' when she forgot them.

'Wasn't there a film' began Em, 'where one of the family was so chirpy and bouncy on a morning that someone used one of her kitchen knives to stab her?'

'Was it an Agatha Christie one?' asked Meg, innocently.

'You had a good night's sleep then?' Raff asked Meg with a grin.

'I did, I slept like a log, although I think I missed most of The Bishop's Wife.'

'And the rest' said Em.

'Did you enjoy the Scrabble?' asked Meg, sitting down and cutting herself a generous slice of the frittata.

'Enjoy?' replied Sadie, eyebrows raised. 'Yes, in a masochistic way I suppose. Em used 'Foggacle' saying it was the mist that appeared on your spectacles when cooking over a hot stove. What were the others?'

'Hekitum.' Raff answered. 'She said it was the Esperanto version of Yorkshire's 'Heckie Thump'

'And don't forget 'Fresn' which is apparently an extremely small black and white cow' laughed James.

'Then there was the karaoke.' Raff said, his eyes raised towards heaven before they settled on the less than angelic Em.

'At least I had a go, unlike two male persons I could mention' she countered.

'I didn't sing because I didn't want everyone discussing it at breakfast, like we are with you' Raff explained.

'I think, possibly the best one was 'Nothing Compares 2 U' in which Em managed to sound less like Sinead O'Connor and more like Rod Stewart with laryngitis' added Sadie and was rewarded with a gasp of indignation from Em.

'And after I helped you out with 'Eight Days a Week' because you mistakenly thought you were singing 'Eight Miles High' and only realised halfway through. Those two were in hysterics' said Em, nodding towards the men who were in hysterics again.

'Oh, I've got a video of that particular duet. Even with Em 'helping' the song is completely unrecognisable' beamed Raff, pulling the phone out to show Meg.

She leaned in towards him and within a few seconds had started giggling – and by the end, both her and Raff were doubled over.

'I deny any responsibility' Sadie said, trying to look affronted. 'It was the karaoke people who put up the wrong words.

'I'm with you pardner' grinned Em 'but you do realise they have blackmail material on that phone for Christmases to come don't you?'

James shook his head.

'Now I realise what sort of family I've married into; I think I may spend next Christmas on a remote desert island.'

'Great – we'll bring the karaoke' smiled Em, evilly.

*

Breakfast was soon finished and bags were packed. Sadie had to just about wrestle the bedding from Meg who wanted to wash it before she went.

'All work is suspended today Meg. Go home and catch up on all the films you want to see and have a day off!' she told her.

'But I'd like to try out my new knives today.' Meg protested.

'Don't look at me when you say that' said Em, 'it makes me nervous.'

All three climbed inside the land rover's front seats after putting the overnight bags and presents in the back, along with some leftover food in plastic cartons. There were lots of hugs and kisses and thank-yous on both sides and then they were on their way. Em insisted on driving so James and Meg braced themselves against the dashboard.

'Let us know what the road conditions are like' Raff shouted over the engine noise 'and I'll let Col know if it's okay to drive to the old cottage today'

'Will do' replied Em as she drove down a driveway that seemed a little more slushy than before.

As they waved them off, Sadie turned to Raff with a sigh. He pulled her in closer to his side as they watched the Land Rover disappear into the lane below.

'I have absolutely loved having them all here. It's been a fantastic first Christmas at Acorn Cottage – apart from those nerve-wracking hours on Christmas Eve of course – but…' She smiled up at him.

'It's nice to be alone, just the two of us?' he asked.

'Exactly. Boxing Day is our day. So no noise, no games, no feasts, no rescues, no climbing slippery, snowy trees to use your phone…'

'I *was* thinking of you' he smiled.

'I know- and I love you for it.'

He bent down and kissed her, his lips hard against her yielding ones, his body pressing against hers. They broke apart.

'Why Raphael, I do believe you're thinking of a little 'anything else we can think of' in the caravan.'

'Only I'd have to get the wood burner going first for the lightweight amongst us and *my* fire might have gone out by then' Raff said, his blue eyes narrowing under the black brows.

'Are you saying you're not aflame for me every minute?'

'When I'm near you, I am on fire every minute. When I'm collecting kindling, getting the fire going, putting on logs and waiting five minutes for it to catch then another five for it to spread warmth around – my ardour may be dampened a little' he grinned.

Sadie thought for a moment. Now was as good a time as any.

'Perhaps we can go up to the caravan anyway. Check inside it and just sit down for a while in friendly companionship?' she said, attempting to be blasé. She didn't want her special 'walking the dogs up the garden at midnight' trip to be in vain.

Raff gave her a strange look, which threw her for a moment.

'Oh well of course, we don't need to go now. We can just…' she stammered.

'No! No, I'd really like to go. In fact, I was going to suggest a walk up there after everyone had gone. Like you said, just to check on things.' Raff finished lamely. He looked nervous, which made Sadie nervous too.

'Shall we take the dogs?' she asked uncertainly.

'Not just now, we'll take them later, shall we?'

Raff leaned in and kissed her again, then gathered her to him, his arm protectively around her as they started to walk up the garden.

Chapter 25

The sun had struggled through this morning, the first time they had seen it for days. It lit up the snow, making it sparkle in different shades of blue, like lots of tiny sapphires had been scattered on it. The trees, still retaining their coating of snow, now glistened as their uppermost branches caught the sunlight.

They reached the fountain with the figure of Brighid looking ethereal in a light dusting of frost. Sadie saluted her as usual. It seemed only right to greet her and she felt sure that Brighid somehow knew of these small tributes.

The gypsy caravan itself showed its bright colours for the first time in a while. It stood out in colourful relief against the stark white background. The thick coating of snow on the roof had begun to melt and the icicles that hung from the roof edges were slowly dripping now.

As they reached the caravan, Raff pulled the key out of his pocket. He really meant it then, thought Sadie, we did intend to bring me up here.

They climbed the steps, unlocked the door and stepped inside. It wasn't too cold after all so Sadie shut the door behind them to preserve what warmth there was. The wood seemed to retain the heat of whatever amount of sun shone onto it and, although she was glad of her thick 'duvet' coat, she wasn't shivering with cold like she thought she would be.

She glanced at Raff. He had on a long, black woollen coat and, as he pushed his black hair out of his eyes, he looked like some sort of romantic, Byronic hero who all the young maidens used to swoon over.

She was worried that the enclosed space would smell musty, not having been used for a while. She sniffed and was rewarded by a pleasant smell of lavender. Raff had learnt from his grandmother that sachets of lavender and other herbs distributed around the place would absorb any smells, emitting their own fragrance at the same time.

Sadie cleared her throat.

'Raff, I'm not sure about this. For you I mean. It's probably not a very manly thing.'

Raff frowned and looked puzzled.

'What's not manly? The caravan?'

'No. I'm probably not explaining this very well' groaned Sadie. 'I've brought you up here to give you your Christmas present.'

Raff's face lit up with a wide smile.

'That's really…weird' he said, shaking his head.

'What is?' It was Sadie's turn to look puzzled as the conversation threatened to run away from her.

'Nothing. Go on.'

'Okay. Well, I made you something. When you thought I was in the study, sewing herb sachets, I was making this. I just thought it was a nod to your ancestry, to your heritage – and I've tried to make it personal' Sadie bit her lip, ran out of words and just indicated the bed under the window at the far end of the caravan.

On it, as artfully arranged as it could be on a freezing cold, midnight visit, was a large patchwork quilt. It sat on top of the eiderdown that was already there but the quilt was thickly padded and heavy enough to keep anyone warm on the coldest nights.

It was made in the same primary colours of reds, blues and yellows, that his mother had used to make the cushions and had the same black outlines. The bright colours were cut and mixed together, the original gypsies just having to use what scraps they could.

In a few central squares, there were depictions of important things in Raff's life. There was the caravan itself taking pride of place. Around it were the log cabin, the barn and Acorn Cottage, as it had played an integral part in the intertwined history of the Norwood and the Maguire families.

There was a simplistic version of Mab's Wood and also a campfire, which Raff loved to light on an evening outside his caravan, just to sit in front of and get back to basics. There was even a square showing Bran, that Sadie had tried to do from a photo. Above the caravan square was one with his name embroidered on it, along with his date of birth.

Raff stood still for a very long time. Taking it all in, leaning forward to see things more clearly, then standing back again. His back was turned towards her and Sadie had no idea what his expression was like. She hardly dared breathe and she realised she was clenching her fists tightly with nerves. He turned towards her, his eyes shining.

'Sadie.' Raff's voice came out in little more than a whisper.' I can't believe you've done all that for me or that you understand so well how important my heritage is to me. The fact that you've studied how gypsy quilts are made is enough but – the personal touches…' he stopped and turned back for a second. He cleared his throat before turning back round.

'It means so much to me Sadie and what means just as much is all the work you put into it for me' and he gathered her in his arms.

'And all the love' she said, her head on his shoulder. 'It had love sewn into every one of those squares.'

She sniffed and he held her so tightly that she could hardly breathe, before releasing her and looking into her eyes. Sadie smiled up at him and then realised something.

'I made it for here but I thought it would look just as good in your log cabin if you wanted to use it there. Now though, if you wanted to transfer it, it would have to be in our pure white bedroom at the cottage. I'm not sure hot gypsy colours would go?'

'Well , you've got your hot gypsy there already – you might as well bring his quilt too' grinned Raff, wiggling his eyebrows suggestively.

'Again, your modesty does you credit' laughed Sadie 'but I have to admit, you *are* hot' and she gave him a full on kiss. She was just going for another when he stepped back.

'Don't distract me' he said nervously. 'I've got your present to give you too, which – in a 'great minds think alike' moment – has been in this drawer since I came up to sort the cabin out for the Blakemores.'

Raff moved past her and reached into the top drawer of a painted cabinet near the door. He came out with a small gift bag and studied it for a moment. Sadie sat down on the padded bench seat opposite. He handed it to her and she took out a small package which was wrapped in silver tissue paper. She started to unwrap it carefully when suddenly, Raff grabbed it back.

'No, I'm not sure you should be doing that. Maybe it should be me? It all depends of course on what the reaction…how it could be construed…I'm not very good at this, am I? I'm just not sure…'

'That's two of us who seem to have lost the power of coherent speech this morning' smiled Sadie 'but you liked my present and I'm sure I'll like yours.'

'It's not even that. I think you'll like the actual present but I'm not sure that you'll like the…' he trailed off again.

'Raff, just give me the present!' she laughed.

He held it out to her but when the tissue paper revealed a small, dark blue leather box, he snatched it off her again. He opened the box, which he held towards her.

Inside was the most beautiful emerald and pearl ring. The square cut emerald in the middle was surrounded, medieval style, with small pearls, all set into gold. Sadie gasped.

'Raff, it's beautiful. How could you ever think I wouldn't like it?'

As she looked up at him, she could feel uncertainty in his face – or was it sheer terror?

'It's because I didn't know what you'd think it was – or even what I think it is' he stammered.

'What do you think it is?' she asked quietly.

'What do *you* think it is?' he replied nervously.

'Well, it's a very beautiful ring' was all she could manage. She didn't want to think too much in case she made a fool of herself. They looked at each other uncertainly for a minute before Raff said,

'Oh god, this is as far from romantic as you can get, isn't it?'

'Romantic?' Sadie repeated, parrot-fashion.

Raff squeezed his eyes shut, opened them again and pulled the ring out of the box.

'I wondered if the thought passed through your mind as to which finger to put it on' he said, reaching for her hand.

Sadie had gradually become aware of what Raff was trying to say- or she thought she was but she had to be sure. She took a deep breath.

'Raff, is this a marriage proposal?'

He swallowed hard and whispered,

'I think so.'

'Talking of being romantic…' she smiled.

'It's just that – ' Raff struggled for words until the right ones came out, tumbling over each other. 'It's just that I have always been my own man and marriage has never meant anything to me. I have always liked the freedom of living by myself. You are as much of a free spirit as I am, we discussed this when we first met – before we got together. We both said we didn't want to be tied down.'

He stopped and looked at her. She *had* said that hadn't she? All she could think of to say now was,

'So – *are* you proposing then?' Shut up Sadie she thought, he'll be running out of the caravan soon. Raff sighed loudly.

'When I first met you, I knew you were different.'

'You tried to chase me off this land with some long-handled pruners' Be quiet Sadie, she thought.

'Be quiet Sadie' echoed Raff, 'let me get through this. It's bad enough as it is. The longer I've spent with you, the more I'm sure that I want to be with you for the rest of my life. So yes, god damn you, will you marry me Sadie?'

213

As he said this, he pulled her up so she was standing inches away from him. She gazed into his eyes without seeing them. She thought of her earlier engagement to someone who had cheated on her. She thought of buying the cottage, the courtyard and therefore her independence. She thought of what he'd said, that she didn't want to be tied down. She thought of all these things in a split second before her eyes came back into focus.

'Oh yes! Yes, I'll marry you!' she cried, flinging her arms round his neck and smothering him in kisses.

Relief flowed out of him and he laughed shakily.

'Well thank god for that. You really put me through the wringer then!'

'I honestly didn't expect it Raff – at all – so I didn't know what my answer would be. I think I've found that out most definitively now though, don't you?'

'Anything less than your full enthusiasm and I'd have thought you were just taking pity on me for losing the power of rational speech'

She laughed crazily, everything seemed heightened at the moment. Things seemed funnier, happier, more perfect and pure than before. But still…

'You *are* sure, aren't you Raff?'

'This is how sure I am' he said, kneeling and taking her left hand in his. As he slipped the ring on her marriage finger, he looked up at her.

'I love you, Sadie Norwood'

'And I love you too Raphael Maguire' and then she burst into tears.

'Don't you dare' he said, standing up and looking stern.

She pointed at her wet cheeks and grinned.

'Happy tears' she squeaked.

Chapter 26

Boxing Day lunch had been forgotten, apart from a small slice of pork pie and a handful of crisps. Raff had hidden one of James' bottles of good champagne in anticipation of the event. If she'd said no, he would have drowned his sorrows with it instead. They were in the throes of toasting each other constantly. It was Raff's turn.

'To the most beautiful, kind, lovely, sexy, intelligent, perfect woman I could ever have expected to be my wife.'

They grinned inanely at each other, crossed arms and then drank out of each other's glasses.

'It's not as easy as it looks in films, is it?' said Sadie, dribbling unromantically down her chin.

'I have never drunk as much champagne as I have this Christmas' said Raff, 'I'm more of a wine man but I could get a taste for this.'

'How many engagements do you plan on having then?' Sadie laughed and then they both smiled stupidly at each other as they realised the next time would probably be their wedding.

'There were births and forthcoming births to toast,' said Raff 'and at some point there will be a wedding and perhaps - well, the cycle continues.'

Sadie blushed, then smiled happily.

'Yes, the cycle continues.'

'Another toast!' said Raff, refilling their glasses.

'My turn now. To the most handsome, insanely sexy, dark and mysterious, wonderful, kind, gorgeous…did I say sexy?'

'My champagne's getting warm.'

To the person I love with all my heart' Sadie concluded, holding her glass up.

'To the only woman I have ever wanted to marry and stay with till the end of time.'

Instead of clinking glasses together, they went for a long breath-taking -literally- kiss.

'Your champagne will definitely be warm now' Sadie laughed.

'Hang the champagne' Raff said, 'I laugh in the face of warm champagne' he said in a ridiculous French accent and they kissed again.

From in front of the Aga, two pairs of eyes watched the human pantomime.

Oh good grief thought Whisky, *How to lose your dignity in one easy lesson.*

You're pleased really thought Bran, ***That means you'll see even more of me as I'll be living here too.***

Can't wait, thought Whisky with heavy sarcasm, *Just remember, I'm the one nearest the Aga when it comes to dog beds.*

Wouldn't dream of displacing you, young man, my breed is hardier than yours.

What do you think then? Love's young dream over there? If I wasn't so comfortable, I'd get up and be sick in a corner in protest at their shenanigans. That should stop them.

You don't mean that but I suppose you can't help being crotchety, it's hard to break the habit of a lifetime. I think it is an excellent match and I thought so right from their very

218

first meeting. You must remember, you were there.

Can't remember much except it was time for my meal and there was this huge black and white monster barking in my ear'ole.

You know I was only obeying orders. Anyway, it's good to think we played our own small part in getting them together. You must be happy for them? Look at them.

Oh for goodness' sake, They're moving in for the kill again. Oh – I suppose I am. They do look happy I suppose. And inebriated. I hope they remember to feed us.

Have you always got to think of your stomach? Where's your sense of romance?

I'm sure it will come back as soon as my feeding bowl is full. I'm pleased for them both and I'm glad you're moving in permanently. Here's to you and me brother.

To us – and to them.

You're not going to try and link paws and drink out of my water bowl instead are you? Those two were slavering down their chins worse than us on a hot day, after a run round the garden.

219

I think not. That's a human thing with the glasses, I've observed it before on the square thing in the living room that has small people on it and sound coming out. The thing that the nice little lady fell asleep in front of last night.

Look. Look at them. They're staring at us with a glazed expression and a silly smile on their faces. What do you think they're thinking?

'Look at those two' laughed Sadie 'hogging the Aga and as happy as Larry. What do you think they're thinking?'

'The way Whisky is giving us the death stare then looking over at his bowl, they're probably thinking we've forgot to feed them.'

'It's not time yet' said Sadie 'but he does look hungry'

'Whisky is *always* hungry; he can eat more than Bran. I suppose we'd better feed them; they only had a few leftovers at breakfast as it was so hectic '

'I'll feed them Raff; you pour the rest of the champagne.'

'You wanton woman. Is alcohol and sex all you can think of?'

'Who mentioned sex? Although – now you *have* mentioned it…'

'Let's finish this off first' Raff said, holding up the glasses. 'It's not every day you get engaged to the love of your life and it's not as though we have anything else to do today'

They did the linking arms and drinking thing again and they both managed to dribble down their chins, oblivious to the look of disgust from Whisky as they did so.

'Do you think we'll get the hang of it by the time we get married?' Raff said.

'Doesn't matter if we spill it. There may be no more champagne but we have other drinks. I could make cocktails – if I had the first idea how to do that. And, like you say, it's not as though we have anything else to do today. The day is our own, We claim it as Raff and Sadie day!'

Then Sadie's phone rang.

Chapter 27

'I am so, so sorry. I am really stupid.
You're having your own precious Boxing Day
and I'm asking favours. I'm an idiot'

'Meg, you can use a scourge for self-
flagellation later if you so wish but there is
honestly no problem' Sadie laughed. 'We will
be there in about twenty minutes as we'll have
to walk. We've both had a liquid lunch'

Sadie laughed at Raff holding up the bottle
of champagne and pulling a drunken face –
eyes crossed and tongue hanging out at one
side.

'So go to the pub to keep warm' she told
Meg 'and we'll meet you there.'

Then she rang Em and asked her and James
to meet them in the pub too, as she wanted Em
to be the first to hear their happy news. Em
explained that Meg had given her a long,

rambling explanation that she couldn't make head nor tail of. Eventually she interpreted that Meg had gone to take some Christmas baking to the old couple down the road and had pulled the door shut behind her, forgetting to take her key. She had rung Em, who said that she had given Meg all her keys and the spare front door one - but Sadie might still have hers. She had said that if not, her and James would come down in striped sweaters and black masks with a jemmy each and they would break in. Luckily, Sadie knew it was on another key ring in the dresser drawer.

Getting dressed up so warm that the Inuit would have been sweating, they set off for Brytherstone. As they came out of the lane and into the road to the village, Col was about to turn up the lane in Raff's van. He stopped and wound his window down.

'That's about the last of the stuff we need now. It was passable, with care, on the roads so I thought I'd give it a try this morning. The rest can go to the tip when the snow clears. The settee, chairs and table are falling to bits and our double bed ended up just being a mattress on the floor after the frame collapsed, so that can go too.'

'I'm glad you've got it all done' said Raff. 'It's still not easy, driving in this lot but it will have a long way to go to beat Christmas Eve.'

'None of us will ever forget that night as long as we live' laughed Col 'nor your bravery'

Raff shrugged it off with a smile.

'And this van. I can't get used to a van that doesn't rattle, squeak or clang and is comfortable to drive' Col said gratefully. 'You have made this family very happy. Please know that.'

'My pleasure' smiled Raff again, looking embarrassed. He hoped Col would soon stop thanking him and just accept it.

'Are you walking into the village? I can turn round and give you a lift?' Col asked.

'It's okay' said Sadie, 'we're quite enjoying our snow-trek. We're getting so used to walking and sliding through snow that it will feel very strange plodding on solid surfaces, where we just walk normally and not as if we're wading through custard. It will be boring so we're making the most of it.'

Col laughed and trundled off with a wave and the last lot of goods from their rented cottage, whilst Sadie put her arm through Raff's and gazed up at him. Her head filled with thoughts about the future as she did. He rewarded her expression of puppy-like devotion with a smile and a kiss that sent the temperature up a few degrees.

As they neared The Falling Stone, they could hear music, laughter and playful shouts, and a general murmur which, as usual on a Boxing Day had increased by ten decibels. Entering the pub, the noise intensified, contrasting sharply with the still quiet and deserted main street outside. The welcome warmth hit them. It was a mixture of log fires and body heat, the place being packed, wall to wall, with what looked like the entire population of Brytherstone.

Sadie gave a little sigh – so much for their quiet, peaceful day at Acorn Cottage with just the two of them. Her eyes searched for Em and James, of which there was no sign. However, Meg fought her way towards them with yet more apologies filling her mouth as she neared them. Sadie put her hand up.

Stop. Now. It's no problem, like I told you and really, I should have given you my key as soon as you moved in but I just forgot about it.'

'I'll give you this back later and I'll get another one cut for Em. I have two keys already in the cottage and I need to know that if I ever lock myself out again, there will be more sensible people than myself within the area who can come to my rescue, like you have today. Did I tell you how grateful I am?'

'Many times Meg' laughed Sadie.

'Can I get you a drink Meg?' asked Raff, battling his way to the bar.

'Lime and soda please Raff'

'Are you sure? I don't want you getting too giddy' he laughed.

'I only had a couple of drinks over dinner yesterday and it knocked me out for the rest of the day' Meg pulled a face.

'I rather think it was all your hard work, the constant, cooking, baking and extra keeping the children occupied that contributed to that.' Sadie hugged Meg and planted a kiss on her cheek.

'I enjoyed every single minute so thank you for including me.'

'You are family Meg' and Sadie remembered how true that was. Every time she had stayed at Em's during school holidays, Meg had been a frequent visitor, along with her late husband. She always arrived with a little treat – a gingerbread man or a crunchy meringue with a chewy middle, filled with cream. She had always called her Auntie Meg when she was young.

'Have you seen Em and James?' Raff asked Meg. He was looking nervous and Sadie smiled. They both wondered what Em's reaction would be.

'No, are they coming down here too?' Meg looked surprised as they hadn't mentioned a trip to the pub when she phoned.

'Yes, we asked them to come here and meet us' said Sadie, giving Raff a significant glance.

The door opened, hardly noticed by the crush of people gathered in the bar. Sadie could just make out the spikes of short red/grey hair and the blond/grey hair next to it over the sea of heads jiggling up and down in conversation.

Em and James were here.

Chapter 28

The five of them huddled around a wooden ledge, which was the only spare place that they could find to stand together.

Sadie was beginning to think that this was a bad idea. If she was to tell them her exciting news, it might take six attempts until they actually heard it – and then, if she had to shout it out in the end, the whole pub might hear it too. Not that she minded that but she had imagined a more intimate gathering. Maybe they could go down the road to Meg's?

Just then, Will Pike and his parents and sister from the newsagents, got up from a table just round the corner from, under the window. Will stood there to save it for Meg and the others. He worked for Meg up at her café at Mab's Court during the holidays and had a soft spot for her.

'Meg, here, grab these seats' he said in the world's loudest whisper obviously worried he would be knocked unconscious in a general stampede to grab the only spare table in the place.

'Oh bless you love.' Meg said as she slid onto a bench seat. Everyone thanked Will and took their places round the table.

'Now' said Em finally, 'as we have half a chance of making ourselves heard now, why did you want to meet us in here?'

'Did we take you away from losing a game of Trivial pursuit?' grinned Raff.

'We've abandoned that as neither of us could answer any of them. We're going to donate it to 'The Society of those born after the year 2000' and buy a special 'Just for old fogeys who can remember things years ago but can't remember where they put their keys yesterday' version. You'd be good at that Meg.'

'I know *exactly* where my keys are. I just forgot to take them with me' Meg protested.

'Still say you'd beat us both, although James *did* start to put tomato chutney on his toast instead of jam this morning.'

'You were distracting me with your dancing around the kitchen' James spoke up in his defence.

'Dancing?' asked Sadie, incredulously.

'Don't worry, it wasn't Salome's Dance of the Seven Veils if that's what you were thinking' Em responded.

'No, it was more Baloo Bear on acid' James said, ducking out of the way to avoid a slap on the head.

There was a silence where they all sipped their drinks.

'Sadie?' said Em pointedly.

Sadie looked up and sighed.

'Shall we all go outside' she said, still too aware of the noise and people around her.

'Whereas normally I'd love to stand with my feet planted in five inches of snow with my nose turning bright red and my fingers ready to drop off... I think today, I'll forego that pleasure' said Em, taking a drink of her whisky.

'Or maybe we could go to Meg's?'

'Sadie' Raff butted in, 'you're just prolonging the agony.'

'Agony? What agony? If it's as bad as all that, tell us after New Year. We've had enough excitement this Christmas' ordered Em.

'Do you want me to…?' Raff began.

'No, I'm getting there' Sadie replied.

'Where?' asked Em.

Sadie took a deep breath and looked round at the expectant faces, looking for enlightenment.

'We just wanted you – all of you – to be the first to know' Sadie was now at a loss. She was just beginning to realise what a big deal this was and she didn't know what to say. Then she felt Raff's hand grab hold of hers, his thumb stroking her fingers. His eyes, when she turned her head, were gazing gently into hers, empathy written there. The simplest way was the best, she thought.

'Raff has asked me to marry him – and I said yes' she announced almost defiantly as though they were all going to condemn her to three days on the rack with thumbscrews an optional extra.

There was a silence of a few seconds, which felt more like an hour, then congratulations sprung from their lips in a torrent of enthusiasm.

Sadie held out her un-mittened hand to show the beautiful ring off to them, which was admired greatly by all.

'I think there is certainly a hex on the Norwood women this year' Em said, 'turning us from independent-thinking women to the chattels of men'

'The day I ever stop you thinking independently is the day when hell freezes over. And, although it feels like it out there at the moment, that day will never arrive. And I thank god for it' said James.

'I have to admit' said Em in a rare moment of non-sarcastic candour, 'that you haven't curtailed my independent spirit in the slightest. I'm very glad I made the right decision in marrying you James.'

He leaned over to bump his shoulder against hers fondly, then stood up to shake Raff's hand, pumping it up and down. Raff once more made his way through the heaving throng to the bar. Using this moment, Sadie whispered across the table,

'Have I done the right thing Em? I know I was happy to be by myself – and still would be – but I didn't count on meeting Raff.'

Em beamed with joy as she said,

'You've done exactly the right thing' then hugged her so that Sadie knew without a doubt that she was happy for her.

'Has *Raff* done the right thing? That's what I ask myself. Marrying a Norwood woman is not a thing to be undertaken lightly.' James said as he and Em looked at each other, their eyes full of love. Suddenly, Sadie could see the future. She knew she had made the right decision. You had to trust in your instincts in the end – as Em had done.

You couldn't draw up a plan of how your future was going to be; how your life was going to unfold. You just had to trust to fate and hope that fate had more of a clue than you did.

Sadie realised that, since the initial congratulations, Meg had been very quiet. She looked across to see her huddled in the corner, tears rolling down her cheeks.

'Oh Meg.' She reached her hand out to cover Meg's 'It's not *that* bad is it?'

'It's very, very good' Meg gulped and gave her a watery smile.

'Are you sure?' asked Em, squeezing Meg's shoulder.

'Of course' sniffed Meg 'It's what we were talking about the other day, isn't it Em? So you know how happy it makes me.'

'Remind me to tell the British Diplomatic Corps never to employ you' muttered Em.

'What's this?' said Sadie with a puzzled expression. 'You were talking about me and Raff getting married?'

Meg stopped sniffing, gave a fleeting glance towards Em and back before the steely gaze had chance to bore into her and then looked at Sadie with wide, apologetic eyes.

'Don't worry' Em replied 'We weren't privy to any inside information. We were just saying how happy you two seemed and we were just wondering if you would end up properly living together. Or even married'

'I said married, Em didn't think you would' went on Meg, like a lamb to the slaughter. She flinched as Em's laser eyes came on full beam in her direction again. She had apparently let

234

out a secret that she had no idea she should keep.

'I didn't factor Raff into the scenario properly. I imagined them both ignoring tradition and doing their own thing – but obviously Raff felt differently.' Em said.

'You couldn't be any more surprised than I am, Em, that he wants to be 'tied down' to a life of hopefully wedded bliss. As for me, I have been against marriage in principle but when it was Raff doing the asking, I abandoned my principles and submitted to him very willingly.'

'You'll never lose your freedom Sadie; we guard it fiercely in this family. Since I finally married James, after years of him asking me, I realised that my freedom to be 'me' was still there – and all I had done was waste the years that we could have been together.'

Sadie hugged Em as regret played across her usually cynical face.

'The important thing' she whispered to her aunt,' is that we are now with the men we love.'

'ANNOUNCEMENT!' came the booming voice of Jez, the landlord, accompanied by the ringing of the brass bell over the bar. 'I would like to announce the engagement of Raff Maguire to Sadie Norwood.'

The place rang with cheers and the thumps of congratulations on Raff's back threatened to cause serious injury.

'Does that mean the drinks are on you, Raff?' some wag shouted from the other side of the bar.

'With this crowd?' came the reply 'I'd need to take a bank loan out.'

He caught Sadie's eye from afar and grimaced apologetically but she just joined in the laughter as she too, received a steady stream of congratulations.

Chapter 29

Raff finally sat down, accompanied by three bottles of Prosecco.

'Jez didn't have any champagne but gave us these free of charge' said Raff, inviting Seth Barraclough and his parents Frank and Sarah over to share their table saying, 'I thought we might need extra help getting through it.'

Seth and his parents laughed as they pulled extra chairs up at the table. They held up their two pints of real ale -Seth and Frank - and half a lager-shandy – Sarah.

'Nay, we'll stick to these thanks lad,' said Frank 'but we'll be pleased to help you celebrate.'

'Seth was the hero of the hour, Mr and Mrs Barraclough. Super-Seth, in fact.' Sadie laughed. 'We might not be celebrating our engagement today but for his actions on Christmas Eve. You must be proud of him.'

Seth's parents looked pleased and proud but also accepting because this was just how Seth always was. How all these old Dales folk had always been. Stoic in the face of danger.

Shelley came to the table with champagne flutes for the Prosecco and another round of drinks for the Barracloughs.

'Ee, I'd better not have too many more of these or I'll never get home' said Frank.

'That's alright Dad, I've got t'trailer on't back to get you and me Mam back' said Seth with such a straight face that Sadie immediately said,

'Oh no. James, could you run Mr and Mrs B…' and then she heard Seth chuckle and saw the others exchanging complicit glances. Seth grinned.

'It's alright lass, we've got makeshift seats across back of tractor cab.'

'Mind you, I'm not saying as a trailer wouldn't be more comfortable' Frank said drily.

'It's okay anyway as I'm not drinking anymore after this and it'll be me as drives t'tractor, so drink yer fill.' Sarah added.

Sadie tried to picture the diminutive Sarah behind the wheel of the tractor and couldn't – but it was obviously part of their Christmas ritual and she probably drove it on the farm anyway. Everyone mucked in and did what they had to.

The afternoon carried on. People left; people joined. Meg, after hugs all round, went back home to watch some Christmas films without falling to sleep and to have a 'nice cup of tea'. Sadie and her table were vying for the 'noisiest table' prize with the Armstrong family. A clatter of glasses on the floor as their table nearly upended and the shouts that ensued, declared the Armstrongs the unofficial winners.

Seth instigated a Hook the Bull game which, to Sadie, looked like a grown-up version of Hoop-la. After watching for a few minutes – she mentally struck out the 'grown-up' before 'version'. The ring was usually hanging from the ceiling on a length of rope which had long since gone. Seth was pitched against Rosie

Armstrong, which, by the look of the primeval flirting that was going on between them, was Seth's secret crush. Rosie looked pretty keen too. When Seth won, he did a little celebration dance that was a cross between a clog dance and the Birdy Song by the Tweets.

Raff easily beat James, prompting Em to tell him to watch the experts as her and Sadie took their turn. Sadie grabbed hold of the ring and completely missed the board. The brown bull with a hook on its nose stared at her balefully.

Now it was Em's turn. She looked down, choosing her place to stand carefully. Her stance was that of a classical Greek statue depicting a discus thrower. She bounced up and down three times and without her eyes ever leaving the board, she let go of the ring. It flew off at right angles to the board and landed perfectly on Jez's head behind the bar.

There was a moment of complete silence then the whole pub erupted in laughter. Jez just stood there with his usual hangdog expression and didn't move. Em stared at him.

'A halo at last Jez, although I'm not sure it suits you.'

Another wave of laughter greeted this and all eyes were now on the contest between Sadie and Em, presumable to see who was the worst shot of the two. Sadie easily won, not least because she manged to actually hit the board. People within 360 degrees, who had moved their drinks out of Em's range, now moved them back.

'How can you carve incredibly intricate features out of stone, which needs a steady hand, yet your throwing skills are abysmal?' Sadie asked.

'I don't know, I've always been like that' replied Em. 'I was once on the school netball team, called in as a last resort. I sized up the hoop. I weighed the netball in my hand – and I threw. It went backwards and hit Mrs Hill, the games mistress who was standing behind me. Struck her square in the face and knocked her false teeth out, which flew across the court to land at my friend's feet.'

Everyone in hearing distance of this was doubled up and tears of laughter were streaming down Sadie's face. Raff appeared by her side.

'Time to go home?' he asked 'It will be dark soon.'

'Spoilsport' answered Sadie – and for the first time, realised that she had drunk more than she should have. She had been carried along on a wave of bonhomie and engagement euphoria. If you can't have a celebratory drink on your engagement to the most gorgeous man on the planet, when can you? She stopped and reined her thoughts in.

'No, it's a good idea Raff' she smiled and reached out for his hand as he smiled back at her.

'Us too, my old harridan' James said ungallantly.

'Just see how he treats me!' said Em with mock annoyance.

'You know I love you to bits' James replied, his hand ruffling her already ruffled hair 'Even if you are a rubbish shot'.

'I let Sadie win; you know'

'Of course you did, my darling' and after fond farewells, they made their exit through a still busy pub.

Raff guided Sadie up to the bar.

'We just wanted to thank you Jez for your engagement present. It went down very well, as you can see.' Raff grinned as he looked towards Sadie. Sadie was wondering if she'd grown two heads before she remembered Meg saying, in one of her wiser moments, that when you're drunk, you always think you're sober – until the next day.

'Yes' she added her thanks, 'it was lovely of you. Unfortunately I think Raff will have to carry me home. Possibly over his back, in a fireman's lift.'

'You're not that bad' said Jez, who, to be fair, had probably seen a lot worse. 'Anyway, you could always take the shorter route.'

Sadie looked puzzled. 'The shorter route?'

'Haven't you heard of it? Goes from behind the pub, as the crow flies, over to Mab's Wood?'

Raff nodded.

'The old footpath. We used it when were younger. My dad used to take me that way to get to the caravan, I remember. Don't think it's used much now is it?'

'I think the Armstrongs used the field for crops instead of pasture so people kept out –

and you probably were driving by then. You can still see the track of it out of the top window after the barley has been harvested though. It's still there.'

'Hidden under several inches of snow…' added Raff ironically.

'It goes from behind the barn, just to the left of it, if you want to give it a go?' said Jez 'It cuts a big corner off.'

'Maybe in summer?' said Raff, silently imploring Jez to keep quiet.

'Is that the barn that the original Bridestone is supposed to be under. The one that gave Brytherstone its name?' asked Sadie, becoming interested. Raff sighed.

'It is.' replied Jez. 'Brighid's Stone was what the village name was derived from.'

'Somebody should get digging to try to find it' she said enthusiastically.

'They have' replied Jez 'Three times over the last seventy years apparently but still no sign. Left me with an unusable storage place for a long period last time so I'm not that keen myself. Anyway, the path's supposed to be a straight line from there to Mab's Wood – and so to Acorn Cottage too.'

'Can we really cut across the fields then?' asked Sadie.

'As I said' Raff replied cautiously 'it *is* a field full of snow.'

'But we'll get back home quicker' she said pleadingly.

'No' said Raff.

'Aw' said Sadie petulantly, bottom lip pushed out.

'Oh god...' said Raff.

'So' she said, giving Raff a victory smirk, 'we just go out the back way and...'

'Straight across in a diagonal line, keeping Mab's Wood in sight as a guide' cut in Jez.

'Thank you Jez.' Raff didn't try to hide his sarcasm. He knew the conversation was leaving him behind.

'Yes!' shouted Sadie, taking this as an agreement 'and it's covered in snow no matter which way we go. Ooh, I'm a poet and I didn't know it.'

She took a deep breath, realising she should try to regain what was left of her dignity and fearing it was too late.

'Seriously' she continued 'if it cuts distance and time, it's good. Besides, it can be our intrepid, Arctic adventure into the wilds, in celebration of our pledging our lives to each other?'

Raff sighed again, defeated.

'When you put it like that, how can I resist?' he said, rolling his eyes. 'Have you got a torch we can borrow, Jez?

Chapter 30

There was still a little daylight left as they walked past the barn and round into the field. The sun was setting, a deep red on the horizon and soon the light would be gone. They were making slow progress through the thick snow of the undisturbed field.

'Keep going, *mo ghraidh*. If we get a move on, we'll be home before dark.'

'But just look at the beautiful sunset' she flung her arm out to the right and smiled beatifically. 'You can't hurry an experience like that. That's one of the lessons you taught me. Practice what you preach.'

'You are quite right and I agree, it is beautiful but if we make it back to the cottage, we can see it in all its glory.'

'Raff, this is a big, open field, we can see it in all its glory from here.'

Raff sighed, gave in and turned round, drinking in the lines of purple and pink radiating on either side of the sun and the diffused light above it. He could almost see the remains of the blazing orb slipping down, inch by inch, changing the sky with every movement. He could never live anywhere built-up. Where he couldn't see the expanses of sky with their amazing displays in the morning and the evening, nor the vast night skies with their stars forming constellations above him.

'You're right Sadie, we should appreciate nature as it happens. It changes so quickly.'

'I'm always right' laughed Sadie and he turned to give her the appropriate, playful response but halted.

'What are you doing down there?' he asked in surprise.

'Sitting' she replied unnecessarily 'and watching the sunset.'

'But what on?' he asked incredulously.

'This stone. At least I think it's a stone. It could be a hippo's bottom sticking up out of the snow. Or a bear's bottom, possibly, as it's furry.'

'What *are* you talking about, you madwoman?' he grinned.

'Feel it' she said, standing up.

Raff went over and stroked the surface of the stone which stood proud of the snow by about fifteen inches and was covered in moss. It was a huge boulder. Or was it a boulder? He vaguely remembered it being there when he was young and standing on it to play 'King of the Castle.

'Sadie, I can hardly believe I'm saying this but, you don't think this could be the Bridestone do you? Here, past the barn, instead of being *inside* the barn? Although, surely the archaeologists would have walked this field, just in case?'

Sadie looked at him, then back at the stone.

'It's a little way from the path as I think we've wandered off piste' he continued ' – and of course, it would be covered by barley or wheat most of the time they were digging in the barn? When the snow has gone, I'll come back and, if it looks like there may be more of it underneath the surface, it might be worth getting Kit Courtney and his team of archaeologists over to have a look. What do you think? It's a stupid idea, isn't it?'

He suddenly noticed Sadie's face as she straightened up from touching the stone with the palm of her hand. She seemed remarkably sober now – and serious.

'It's not a stupid idea at all. I think you should do it. I think you could be right.'

Raff knew then that she had felt something. A connection. She had these epiphanies occasionally, which she blamed on her ancestors.

A change in the air made him look across the field again. The sun had almost disappeared.

'Right, plenty of time to think about that another day. For now, let's just get home.'

He linked his arm through hers and they started off in the direction of Mab's Wood again. As they got nearer, he could see his cabin lit up at the windows and felt nothing but pleasure that it was being used and filled with people.

If he followed a definite 'as the crow flies' route from the barn, this would bring them out more to the back of the Acorn Cottage garden.

Unfortunately, there was a deep ha-ha between the garden and this field, so it would be better to go to the caravan clearing, where he knew they could jump the smaller ditch more easily.

He veered off to the right, dragging Sadie who was trying to turn around to catch the last of the twilight sky behind them. He came to the place where the gap was at its narrowest.

'Sadie. Sadie! Look at me. We're going to jump over this ditch, then we're in the caravan clearing.'

He shone the torch to show her exactly where he meant.

'Okay, no problem' beamed a happy Sadie, which only succeeded in convincing Raff that it *would* be.

'Just grab my hand. Together now. One, two -three…'

They both flew over the ditch and landed in the clearing. Raff on two feet, Sadie flat out on her stomach.

'Sadie! Are you alright?' Raff bent down to her in genuine concern.

A giggle could be heard as she lifted her head out of the snow, which helped allay Raff's fears. Then, as she started moving her legs and

arms in and out, he knew she was okay. Crazy –
but okay. He started laughing as he watched her
moving her limbs slowly.

'What *are* you doing?' he asked, not sure if
he needed to know the answer.

'I'm making a snow-angel. In the snow.
Obviously' she giggled again.

'Of course you are' Raff was still laughing.
'Aren't you supposed to do that on your back?'

'I'm an upside-down snow-angel and the
results will be the same.'

She turned her head and grinned up at him
as he pulled her out of the snow.

'Let's get you back quickly and out of
those wet clothes.'

'You naughty boy – just can't wait, eh?'

'Sadie – you're going to catch your death
of cold'

'Okay mother, lead on.'

They reached the terrace at the back of the
cottage and Raff unlocked the French door of
the kitchen at the back, thankful to feel the heat
from the Aga that greeted them as they stood on
the threshold.

'Hot chocolate?' he asked.

'Mm, that would be lovely.'

'Aren't you coming in?' he asked as she hesitated.

'I thought I'd stay out here for a few minutes. It's so beautiful.'

'You really need to keep moving' said Raff, his brow furrowing.

'I'll run round a bit then' she offered, fully aware that she still wasn't quite sober and hoping that might help. She had certainly revived a little though since that full-length dive into the snow, it had to be said. Also, that strange feeling that had emanated from the stone as she touched it, had sobered her up too.

She went back down the steps onto the snow-covered grass and started to run in circles. Raff looked up through the window as he filled the kettle and cracked up. Crazy lady, he thought. Which was, of course, one of the many reasons why he loved her.

Whisky and Bran ran out to join her and followed her round in circles.

Strange rituals these humans have, running round in circles in brass monkey weather, thought Whisky.

As if you don't do the same thing, chasing your tail even though you know you'll never catch it, thought Bran.

This is like a game of follow my leader.

There is no leader in a circle.

Wow, a great truth, O Wise One!

I suppose it gives them a bit of exercise as well.

I don't know about you but that's my exercise for the night. I'm off back in to get warm. What about you, my partner in crime?

I'm with you, compadre.

Sadie watched them both run back into the warm house. At least they've had a bit of exercise, she thought. She sighed deeply and happily. What a wonderful first Christmas at Acorn Cottage. She couldn't have wished for anything more. Although she was glad Raff hadn't ended up with hypothermia, or worse. It could have turned out badly but it didn't, so she put those thoughts away.

She sat on the terrace wall and looked up at the stars, spreading now over a clear night sky. Could nature be any more beautiful than this exquisite display she was seeing tonight? To her left, the bright moon shone through the

254

branches in all its transient glory, creating light and shadow on the trees bordering the garden.

She could see Brighid, catching the moonlight on her serene, all-seeing face. She looked down at the ring, almost hidden in the darkness but feeling just right on her finger.

There was a hand on her shoulder. Raff pulled her up and kissed her, gently, lovingly – and then they both turned towards the warmth of Acorn Cottage and shut the door behind them.

There was a movement at the edge of the trees. A pair of beautiful, intense, *knowing* eyes, missing nothing, glinted in the moonlight - and a graceful, pale creature turned and made its way back through the trees, towards Mab's Wood.

*

Thank you for reading Acorn Cottage Christmas. I hope you enjoyed this festive offering? If you did, please leave a review if possible.

This is a stand-alone book but the characters are from my earlier book, The Gypsy Caravan. If you would like to know more about them and their back story, including how Sadie brought Acorn Cottage back into the family- the book and e-book are available on Amazon.

There are a few things that might need to be explained.

-Mo Chridhe means My Sweetheart

-Mo Ghraidh means My Darling

-Mo Chroi means My Heart

-Cailin means Girl

They are all from the Gaelic language.

- A Ha-ha is a deep ditch or sunken wall, used to keep livestock out whilst preserving an open view over the countryside.

258